©Shingo Adachi

Date: 3/12/19
GRA
Kagy
Gobl
Year
D0096139
PALM BEACH COUNTY
LIBRARY SYSTEM
3650 Summit Boulevard
West Palm Beach, FL 33406-4198

1

GOBLIN SLAYER

SIDE STORY: YEAR ONE

©Shingo Adachi

The words she meant to say to him when she got back. The place she could never return to.

She couldn't go home. She hadn't gone home, and she never would.

©Shingo Adachi

“I’ll be waiting,
so this time—
this time—”

What's it
to me?
©Shingo Adachi

Let one village be destroyed;
the world would go on.
Let one man die; the world
would keep turning. The dice
would continue to be cast.

Contents

©Shingo Adachi

GOBLIN SLAYER

SIDE STORY: YEAR ONE

VOLUME 1

KUMO KAGYU

Illustration by
SHINGO ADACHI

GOBLIN SLAYER

SIDE STORY: YEAR ONE

VOLUME 1

KUMO KAGYU

Translation by Kevin Steinbach ❧ Cover art by Shingo Adachi

This book is a work of fiction. Names, characters, places, and incidents are the product of the author's imagination or are used fictitiously. Any resemblance to actual events, locales, or persons, living or dead, is coincidental.

GOBLIN SLAYER GAIDEN: YEAR ONE volume 1
Copyright © 2018 Kumo Kagyu
Illustrations copyright © 2018 Shingo Adachi
Original Character Design © Noboru Kannatuki
All rights reserved.
Original Japanese edition published in 2018 by SB Creative Corp.
This English edition is published by arrangement with SB Creative Corp., Tokyo in care of Tuttle-Mori Agency, Inc., Tokyo.

English translation © 2018 by Yen Press, LLC

Yen Press, LLC supports the right to free expression and the value of copyright. The purpose of copyright is to encourage writers and artists to produce the creative works that enrich our culture.

The scanning, uploading, and distribution of this book without permission is a theft of the author's intellectual property. If you would like permission to use material from the book (other than for review purposes), please contact the publisher. Thank you for your support of the author's rights.

Yen On
1290 Avenue of the Americas
New York, NY 10104

Visit us at yenpress.com ☆ facebook.com/yenpress ☆ twitter.com/yenpress ☆ yenpress.tumblr.com ☆ instagram.com/yenpress

First Yen On Edition: October 2018

Yen On is an imprint of Yen Press, LLC.
The Yen On name and logo are trademarks of Yen Press, LLC.

The publisher is not responsible for websites (or their content) that are not owned by the publisher.

Library of Congress Cataloging-in-Publication Data
Names: Kagyū, Kumo, author. | Adachi, Shingo, illustrator. | Steinbach, Kevin, translator.
Title: Goblin Slayer side story year one / Kagyu Kumo ; illustration by Shingo Adachi ; translation by Kevin Steinbach.
Other titles: Goblin Slayer gaiden year one. English
Description: First Yen On edition. | New York : Yen On, 2018–
Identifiers: LCCN 2018027845 | ISBN 9781975302849 (v. 1 : pbk.)
Subjects: LCSH: Goblins—Fiction. | GSAFD: Fantasy fiction.
Classification: LCC PL872.5.A367 G5613 2018 | DDC 895.63/6—dc23
LC record available at https://lccn.loc.gov/2018027845

ISBNs: 978-1-9753-0284-9 (paperback)
978-1-9753-0285-6 (ebook)

10 9 8 7 6 5 4 3 2 1

LSC-C

Printed in the United States of America

GOBLIN SLAYER

SIDE STORY: YEAR ONE

VOLUME 1

PROLOGUE

Campaign Climax

Thus, the World Was Saved

The horizon was filled with darkness; the setting sun's crimson blaze illuminated a misshapen horde. A breeze carried the stench of rot across the field.

Zombies, ghouls, skeletons, and wraiths alongside grinning alter-planar demons, their lips dripping foul liquid.

It was an army of the undead. An army of the dark.

The advancing host represented the gravest possible threat to the forces of Order.

A young crown prince, confronted with this army of Chaos, rubbed his stiff hand. The diamond equipment he carried was light as a feather, so it must have been born of nervousness.

The army of the Prayer Characters had spread itself out across a small hill, and this prince was one of its generals. From the foot of the hill, he looked back, casting a glance over his assembled companions. As they waited anxiously for his signal, the prince, as their leader, had to turn back and face the devils approaching them.

Whether they had any hope of winning was not the question.

Victory was their only option.

Above all, though, it was not they themselves who would determine the course of this battle. All those gathered on this field were nothing more than helpers, assistants to the one who would save the world.

They were prepared to die in the endeavor...

"Your Highness! Your Highness! Everyone's ready!"

The voice that shook him out of his reverie was incongruously cheerful. In the midst of the formation, he could see a young person, small in stature. It was the captain of the self-proclaimed Rhea Brigade, a group of volunteers. The prince couldn't suppress a hint of a smile.

"Is that right? Well, we'll be prepared for them whenever they arrive, then."

"Yes, I think so," the rhea said. "The elves and the dwarves are a little nervous. The lizardmen looked downright happy, though," the rhea added, then offered a small smile.

"Battle is the greatest joy they know," the prince said. "Heartening allies to have in combat."

"True enough, that. If you're all so kind as to fight on our behalf, then at the very least we can manage a bit of running around."

Rheas had an almost magical ability to make themselves invisible, and for the moment, their usual nonchalance had vanished. They were serving as excellent messengers here on the battlefield. It would have been foolish to take the little people, brave though they were, and pit them against the enemy.

When the prince said as much, though, the rhea inquired with a chuckle, "But what will you do if there's an enemy you humans can't kill?"

Still, they were well suited to the communications role the prince had assigned them. There was no one else who could so skillfully sneak across a battlefield filled with flying magic and the clash of weapons, undetected and unafraid.

I've got to admire the rheas, he thought.

"Right, then. Tell everyone that we'll start on my signal. Just as planned."

"No changes? All right, then."

As soon as the short exchange ended, the rhea vanished. No race in the world could match them in sheer talent to become invisible.

Upon deeper reflection, the prince thought to himself that humans were no match for the elves when it came to bows, or the dwarves and their axes, or even combat in general when compared to the lizardmen.

Simply put, the prince was only general of the human forces. The elves, dwarves, lizardmen, and rheas had gathered here strictly out of goodwill. And the prince was deeply grateful for it. He took a deep breath, then rose from his folding stool.

"Have you prepared Turn Undead? We want to give those wretches a proper greeting."

"Indeed, Your Highness," answered an old woman, the high priestess of the God of Knowledge. She was hardly of an age to be on the battlefield, yet here she was with her head held high. "But those creatures," she said, "they aren't cursed. It's something more like an illness. As if they were already on the cusp of returning to dust..."

"I figured as much. Very well."

The prince took in a breath and let it out. His hand closed, then opened.

"Troops... The scales are ruthless. The dice, even more so. No one can say what our destiny is."

The leaders and staff in the camp silently turned toward him. A royal magician used one of his spells—precious, yet at this moment, wholly appropriate—to weave an enchantment that carried the prince's voice on the wind. The army of Order would hear their leader's impassioned words clearly.

"It may be that Order will one day be destroyed. That all will burn, and we will be forgotten."

As the prince's voice rose, he took the reins of his beloved horse. He put his feet in the stirrups and lifted himself into the saddle. It had been so long since he had done so, he had feared he had forgotten how. He took a breath.

He glanced to either side: the royal guard, dressed in a jumble of various equipment, were grinning at him. They were all young, of different races and social classes drawn from different branches of the military, united only by the patina of grime that seemed to cover them all. No one would have assumed they were handpicked elites.

You lot, the prince thought with a chuckle, then lowered the diamond visor of his own helmet. These were his comrades, companions with whom he had navigated mazes, won citations for martial valor, and who had finally coalesced around him as his guard.

Good gods. This is nothing like an adventure.

"Just don't forget, the same is true of our opponents. The dice are merciless—but fair."

On this side, there was a great army with only themselves to rely on. Across the field were as many monsters bent on consuming the earth.

The prince took it all in, then offered his final exhortation:

"There is indeed hope for victory. We must seize it!"

A lusty battle cry went up, so passionate and proud that the creatures squirming on the horizon took an involuntary step back.

Gear clanged and throats shouted themselves hoarse. The army worked up their morale with a great stomping on the ground.

Down with demons! Down with Chaos! We're going to knock you into the next dimension!

"Miracles!"

The first order. The clerics who peppered the battle line began to offer up their prayers to the gods.

O you many gods, who are seated in heaven. Please, protect us. Be our salvation. Grant us victory, we implore.

Protection, Blessing, and Holy War shone out. Miracles came from every god: the Supreme God, the Earth Mother, the God of Knowledge, the God of Trade, as well as the God of War.

The prince nodded. No doubt the forces of Chaos were relying on the dark abilities of their own evil deities.

"Archers, ready the first volley!"

Human hunters, along with the ranks of experienced foresters provided by the king of the elves, drew their bows with a collective tremor of string.

They aimed up, at a diagonal. The humans grimaced, intently focused, but the elves never lost their easy smiles. Why should they? They spent every waking moment with their bows. Shooting was as simple as breathing.

"Loose!!"

The elven arrows went three times faster, higher, and farther than the human ones. They traced a great arc through the sky, then came down like rain upon the forces of Chaos. Their silver arrowheads would be certain to damage even the undead.

At the same time, there was a fluttering sound from the army of the Dark Gods, as of many ragged cloths flapping at once. Dark shadows, dancing in the sky, were deflecting the hail of arrows:

Giant bats.

They spread their massive wings like a canopy over their allies' heads, horribly loyal to their evil friends. The bats fell with a cacophony of shrieks, but thanks to them, damage to the enemy forces was minimal.

Had Order just been forced to waste ammunition? Or had they whittled away some of the enemy's airpower? Of course, the prince would view things in the latter way.

"How stupid do you have to be to leave the good, solid ground?" the prince muttered, and the adventurers of the royal guard smirked at one another.

A little humor was a good thing; it kept one relaxed. Just one of many pearls of wisdom the prince had picked up while adventuring.

"All right, keep going! Spell casters, unleash your magic!"

They had the initiative. They couldn't let the enemy find an opportunity to strike back.

The royal magicians brandished their staffs and began intoning words of true power in loud, clear voices.

Fireball was the favored spell. A volley of them went flying at the enemy. The spheres of flame burned white-hot as they flew, exploding among the ranks of the foe. There was a vast noise, and enemy soldiers went flying into the sky like twigs, torn to pieces.

It was clear, though, that the effect was not as dramatic as it normally would have been. The humans weren't the only ones who could prepare their defenses.

Insofar as they were ones with the underlying logic of magic, the evil gods might even have had an advantage…

"DEEEEEVLLLIIIVVVVVIL!!"

And at last, the Dark Gods saw fit to make their move.

No sooner had the unearthly noise sounded than a swarm of

hard-carapaced bugs assaulted the forces of Order, falling like a hail of pebbles. There was an earsplitting sound of wings as the insects flew, then crashed into the holy barrier. Most were stopped by the divine miracle, but more than a few broke through. In the blink of an eye, foot soldiers, knights, archers, wizards, and monks were riddled with holes, many dying.

"Steady!" the prince shouted, waving his sword even as one of the insects glanced off his helmet. "Vanguard, charge!"

The knights gave their steeds their head and, with a great bellow, went on the attack. The noise of hooves rattled the ground.

At the same moment, there was an eerie *wha-pum, wha-pum* of war drums, and the lizardman skirmishers launched into battle.

These two units were seemingly polar opposites, yet in fighting prowess, they were almost indistinguishable.

"DAAAAEEEMMEMMMEMMEOOOON!!" came the Dark Gods' cry.

The enemy army had recovered from the fireballs, and now a contingent of dullahans rode forth. The combined speed of the oncoming horses, along with the total weight of their riders, lent the knights' spears enough force to knock down a castle wall. Their collision on the battlefield created a virtually indescribable noise of combat.

The screech of metal on metal rang out, and horsemen on both sides went flying. Spears pierced clean through shield and armor alike, while others fell from their horses to suffer broken bones or to be trampled by their own mounts.

Corpses littered the battlefield in an instant, but of course, it was the end of nothing.

"Ahh! Behold, behold! I am a fang, the descendant of Archaeopteryx!"

The lizardmen swooped among the enemy like shadows, eliciting screams from first one villainous creature and then the next. Claw, claw, fang, tail. The sons of the nagas knew no fear; their conduct in battle was irreproachable before their forefathers. They howled out that the fire that fell from heaven had already taught their people of destruction eons ago.

Yet, the vigor of the dullahans, having broken through the knights' charge, was likewise undiminished. They waved spears encrusted with blood; it looked like they would simply overrun the entire army.

"Spear wall, ready!"

It was the job of the foot soldiers to prevent that from happening. Lined up in three rows, they plunged the butt ends of their lances into the ground, creating a three-tiered wall of spears.

Normal horses might have feared the pointy barrier, but the pale and evil mounts of these riders did not. Irritated by the obstacle in their way, the dullahans brandished their weapons. The spears were quickly cut down at the shafts, and next, the spearmens' heads began to go flying…

"Yaaaah! All in, troops!"

That was when the dwarven shield breakers appeared. The hooks they carried caught the dullahans' shields and pulled them away, whereupon the dwarves' battle-axes came into play.

Ax and war hammer swung, crushing and smashing. Fearless, undaunted, wave upon wave broke forth, shoring up the battle line. The meaning of the term *dwarf fortress* became clearly evident.

Can we win?

Who could blame the prince for the passing thought? If all went well, there was no doubt. Yes, the forces of Order might be considered to have the upper hand to this point.

But oh, wait and behold.

The Dark Gods chanted their spells, and a fell wind began to blow over the battlefield. The soldiers who encountered the miasma found that their flesh and organs rotted and dropped away even as they lived; they collapsed writhing to the ground. There was no question: they were being turned into the undead.

When bitten by a zombie, eaten by a ghoul, or when one's soul is frozen by a wight, it's as if one becomes their own tormentor. Those who die in battle should rightly return to the earth, but instead they were being incorporated into the enemy ranks as undead warriors.

The longer the battle went on, the more the forces of Chaos would consume and grow. A true "dawn of the dead" might not be so far away…

"Stay steady! Those aren't the men you know! Destroy them, and give your comrades-in-arms back their bodies!" the prince shouted, but the beginnings of panic were written on his face.

Ranged to the right and left of the prince were his handpicked knights. If they could only break through and surround the Dark Gods, the situation might be salvaged…

But how many knights would have to die to achieve that? Would they, too, become undead?

The answers to those questions would affect more than just this battle. When the fighting was over, how would he find new people? How could the land be made fertile again? How could the towns be brought back?

They might win the battle, but could they really save the world?

"……"

Stop.

Even the gods didn't control the pips on the dice, much less a mortal.

The prince gave a violent tug on his horse's reins. He would start with what was in front of him. It bothered him, deeply disturbed him, to know that he could not finish this through his own wisdom and talent alone.

The course of this battle depended on six people who were far away.

The adventurers delving the Dungeon of the Dead.

§

High Priestess opened her eyes when she heard the leader say it was about time to go.

No—*opened her eyes* wasn't quite the right expression. It had been a long time since she had seen anything but darkness.

Things have probably started up above, the leader murmured, inspecting a weapon.

The overflowing miasma, the sensation of the cold flagstone, the crushing sense of menace. She could remember the break they took in the hallway between burial chambers like it was yesterday.

She heard the faint, familiar clacking of the leader's armor. No doubt he was inspecting his cleaver, just like usual.

"Are you all right?"

High Priestess was pulled back to herself when someone suddenly spoke to her.

It was Female Wizard. She was the daughter of a well-to-do family, and her gentle voice reflected her breeding.

"Yes, fine," High Priestess replied with alacrity, so as not to worry her solicitous companion. She rose.

"Well, if you need anything, let me know. *That* boy doesn't understand the first thing about what a girl wants."

High Priestess dismissed Female Wizard's customary condescension toward the leader. The way the wizard responded by pouting, her cheeks puffed out, made her seem infantile and unreliable.

But as the leader of the back row, with command over the use of spells, everyone trusted her. High Priestess included, of course. And she was genuinely grateful that Female Wizard was willing to watch over her. She could overlook a little bit of peevish behavior…

"Well, she does have to decide whether to go forward or back, after all. It won't do to stray far from the elevator."

This quiet advice must have been offered by Bugman Monk. It wasn't unusual to have two religious types in a single party. Bugman Monk always spoke carefully, perhaps because he was the oldest and most experienced member of the group. "In the fight that's about to start, anyone who's less than totally prepared would only be a burden."

High Priestess didn't wholly approve of his brusque tone, but they had known each other a long time. She smiled faintly.

She could hear a rustle as the bugman unrolled the map he had made and traced a path with one long claw.

"We're about halfway along. We can continue down to the tenth floor or go back. I don't mind either way."

"Since we've been conservin' our spells so carefully, we should still have a li'l leeway, right?" Half-Elf Thief sounded like the darkness of the labyrinth didn't bother him at all. Uncharacteristically for a thief, he was standing on the front row, but he gave no indication of being tired. Or perhaps, like High Priestess, he was just hiding it.

Still, his cheerful tone lifted her own spirits, and for that, she was grateful.

©Shingo Adachi

"Then 'gain, vitality and endurance are different things. Won't do us no good if our hearts ain't in it. How 'bout a little more rest?"

"What's this? Tired already? Hee-hee!" Female Warrior laughed meaningfully and playfully jabbed at Half-Elf Thief with her spear.

In conventional terms, Female Warrior was probably the most attractive of the three women in the party, and it was because of the tragedy in her past. High Priestess knew this, because she had experienced something similar. What was more, High Priestess thought Female Warrior incredible, because she never let her past show through.

"Well, that just won't do," Female Warrior was saying. "Don't you want the girls to like you?"

"Aww, shaddup."

So when Female Warrior whispered, "Right?" to her, High Priestess had to giggle.

It had taken time, but now they were all fast friends. They could never have survived the adventure that led them to this point if even one of them had not been there.

"What about you?"

"Wha?"

High Priestess cocked her head at the unexpected voice. The leader, who had been silently listening to their collective discussion, had suddenly turned the talk to her. "What about you?"

"I, uh..."

It was always this way. He looked lackadaisical, but he was considerate toward all of them. He would never make a decision based on just one person's input but would make certain he had heard from everyone.

If not...how could I ever have followed him this far?

She had been able to reach this point precisely because of her companions. They had waited until she could rejoin them. Just as even now, they waited to hear her words.

"Let me see... There may not be a next time." Thus, she had grown able to confidently offer her own opinion. "Personally, I want to finish this now."

When he spoke, the party looked at one another and all nodded. *Then let's go.*

"A final showdown with the Big Bad, huh? I like it. Can't wait!"

"Heh! Heh! Heh! Heh! If that Demon Lord comes at me, I'll chop him into tiny pieces!"

"Great. Then if we lose, it's your fault."

"Aw..."

"It'll be all right. We all trust one another."

We'd damn well better. The leader gave Female Wizard a wry smile and started walking.

High Priestess followed after him, clutching the scales and sword between her still-developing breasts.

She didn't know how many of them would survive or how badly they would be hurt in this fight.

Every single one of those doing battle above might die.

But...

The world would be saved. Of that, she was sure.

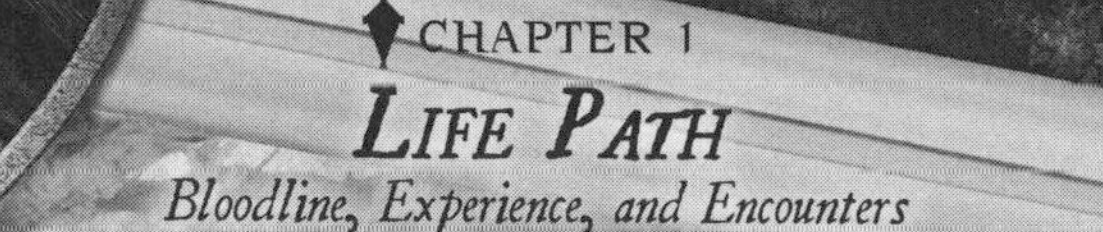

CHAPTER 1

LIFE PATH

Bloodline, Experience, and Encounters

It had been three days since his older sister had ceased to exist. That was why he decided to move.

His sister had told him absolutely not to move from where he was, but she was no longer his sister, any more than a hunk of steak was a living cow. No more than sausage was a pig, or an egg was a chick, or a chick a full-grown chicken. A chicken was neither its meat nor its egg.

The boy, only just turned ten, crawled carefully out from between the floorboards where he had been hiding. His pants were wet with his own excrement and unpleasantly itchy, but it was nothing he couldn't endure.

More pressing was the pain of his stiff joints, and the agonizing effort of trying to keep the floorboards from squcaking. The clamor of the invaders was more distant now, thankfully, but still, there was no substitute for caution.

His sister had told him that he was always hungry, yet strangely, he didn't notice the emptiness of his stomach now. Perhaps it was the mud he had stuffed into his mouth to prevent his stomach from growling at the charred aroma of those he had once loved. She had taught him that the soil here was edible, and that in times of famine, people sometimes ate it.

His throat was as prickly and dry as the days in high summer when he had played until noon; his head thundered with pain, his temples throbbing to the beat of his heart with a great, deep ache as if they were being struck repeatedly.

He didn't bother to glance around the room as he scuttled over the floor toward the kitchen. A soup pot had been overturned, and a kitchen knife was missing. The water jug was shattered, but the bottom of it was still intact.

He leaned over it like a dog, slurping down all he could before he had to come up for breath. If he had known that simple water could be so delicious, he would never have begged his sister to add sugar to his drinks.

Then, finally, he sat down on the floor, not even taking the time to wipe his mouth as he looked around the inside of the house.

The dresser was in splinters, a violent mess, his sister's clothes pulled out and scattered everywhere. Among the debris, he spotted the ribbon he had given her for her birthday. There were marks from little bare feet trampling all over it.

Their father's bow, which had hung on the wall, was broken; their mother's medicine bag had been torn apart and then thrown aside.

When was it that our parents disappeared?

He tried to remember what their mother and father had looked like, but as usual, he could summon only hazy images. His father, a ranger, and his mother, a medicine woman, had (so he was told) died in an epidemic before he was old enough to really remember them. His mother, insistent on caring for others, had caught the disease herself; and his father, who had been in the wilderness looking for something savory, had likewise fallen ill.

After that, it was his older sister who raised him.

And he had watched until the very end what had happened to her.

He braced himself against a ruined bedframe and slowly rose.

The room was a shambles, covered in mud and blood and something sticky.

Somehow, it just didn't feel right. But why? He cocked his head, mystified, but it came to him immediately:

This was no longer his house. This house was no longer his home.

He sought out the treasure chest hidden beneath the bed. The lid was smashed and someone had rifled through the contents. It had contained the pretty stones he'd found while playing with the girl next door, some pressed dry flowers, and a stick that was the perfect size to be a sword.

Now all of it was destroyed, stolen, lost.

Fishing through the box, he thought he had grabbed hold of his father's dagger. It was a memento of his, with a hawk's-head hilt, entrusted to the boy by his sister.

But all he could find was the dagger's scabbard, and he tossed it back into the box.

When he went to leave the house, he felt something through the bottom of his shoe.

It was his sister's purse. It was just a plain leather pouch, but it was sewn with a flower pattern. He took it in hand and heard the faint jangling of coins inside.

He tugged on the string and then hung the purse around his neck, tucking it inside his shirt. He made sure to close the purse tightly so that it would make no sound.

Slowly, he peeked out the door, making certain that *they* weren't around, and then went outside.

The sky was a gruesome reddish black. Was it morning or evening? He couldn't tell.

His shadow stretched out, and he stuck close to the wall of the house to conceal it, as if he were playing a game of shadow stepping. Eventually, he made it far enough along the wall to get a glimpse of the house next door. Not that he needed to look.

Hanging from the branch of a tree in their yard, where there had once been a swing he liked to swing on, were the bodies of the husband and wife who had lived there.

Other than his sister, it was the one thing he had been able to see in the past three days.

He hardly felt anything about it, though, as they no longer looked human to him.

What about her, *I wonder?*

He struggled with whether to look for her but soon realized it was a question he didn't need to answer. If she had come back, it would have been by carriage, and the wreck should be around somewhere. If there was no carriage, it meant none had arrived.

It meant everyone knew this village had been attacked by goblins. Everyone knew, and no one had come.

He could hear excited voices in the distance. The crackling of a campfire. The sounds of cooking.

He clenched his fist and bit his lip, but no matter how hard he dug his nails into his hands, no matter how hard he bit down, he couldn't make them bleed; it was so terribly frustrating.

If *they* had known he was standing here now, thinking these thoughts, they would only have laughed at him. That was all there was to it. By the time they attacked the next village, they would already have forgotten about him.

I should get out on the town road.

He had never been to town. He had no idea how far it might be or whether it was even possible to walk there.

But it felt like his only choice.

Then, suddenly, his knees buckled, and he stumbled. It seemed he didn't have the strength to stand.

But I must...go forward...

He began to crawl along the ground, forcing his body to move toward the road. His elbows and knees got scraped raw, but he ignored them and kept moving.

He crawled single-mindedly down pathways, through bushes, past places he had been running happily around until just days earlier. He ignored the useless thoughts that bubbled unbidden into his mind; he focused on keeping his arms and legs moving.

A long time passed.

His surroundings gradually grew dark, which meant that perhaps the red sky earlier had been twilight. He didn't bother to look up from the mud, even as stars came out overhead and the twin moons began to shine above him.

Soon, he would be at the fence that marked the border of the village. The one he and that girl had once snuck up to, only to be roundly scolded by his sister. If he could get past that fence, he would be outside.

It would be the first time he had ever left his village, and it would be because his village had been destroyed by goblins.

"GROBB...!"

"GOOBRRB! GRO!"

But it seemed things would not be so simple.

There they were.

They weren't that much taller than he was, as if they were just some brats from a neighboring village. But they were far, far more terrible.

He knew because he had seen every minute of what they'd done.

He knew why these creatures, normally reputed to dress in rags, had fresh, new outfits this evening.

They were standing listlessly around the fence, spears in hand. Even the boy could tell they were guards. He had seen the adults in his village trading off the watch at the village gate, so he knew what a guard was.

Were there other paths that led out of the village? He tried to think, but his mind was hazy, and it was difficult. There were a few side streets he had discovered while playing, but he couldn't imagine the goblins hadn't found them as well.

He breathed as quietly as possible, trying to stay hidden, but suddenly, a pair of the little burning pupils turned in his direction.

He sees me.

The boy learned then that goblins could see in the dark, although the knowledge came too late to help him.

He grabbed a stone in his right hand and stood. He threw the stone. It might have been nighttime, but he had the light of the moons and the stars. The rock whistled through the air in an arc.

"GOBORR?!"

The goblin screamed, accompanied by a wet crunching sound. He tumbled to the ground, writhing, blood streaming from his nose. He clutched his hands to his face and made a sort of panicked whine.

Forcing his shaking legs to move, the boy picked up another rock and started running.

"GOOBRBRRB!"

The remaining goblin had been laughing at his companion's misfortune, gesturing at him with his spear.

The boy knew he wouldn't make it in time, but he didn't care.

Now the other goblin, gibbering with rage, picked up his spear.

Die, you filthy monster, the boy thought. He gripped the stone as hard as he could.

The rusty spear tip rushed at him. It was clear to him that this would be the end. The only real question was whether the end would come here, immediately, or over the next several days…

"I see now."

At that moment, there was a gust of cold wind from the west, such as the kind that blows at night.

He didn't understand what had happened; he only registered a whistling, like a flute. Then the heads of the goblins in front of him went flying, and the sound changed to spurting blood.

He used his sleeve to wipe away the dark blood that splattered on his face. His older sister was no longer there to scold him for bad manners.

"The boy's got nerve, if nothin' else."

At that moment, he thought he saw a hideous, wrinkled old rhea.

But no sooner had he registered the sight than a dull, heavy pain lanced through his head, and his darkness overcame his consciousness.

It was not until he came to that he realized he must have been knocked out.

And the end hasn't come yet.

§

Another village destroyed by goblins.

It would never be anything more than another number in another report furnished to the king, who would never so much as know the village's name.

Perhaps not even the gods knew what the village was called…

INTERLUDE

Of Something Typical That Becomes the Seed of an Adventure

The sharp sound of metal echoes through the tunnel today, as it does every day.

Down and down they go, deeper and deeper into the ground, seeking the metal they desire.

Human and dwarf miners, diggers of all races, break the rocks with pickaxes, tunneling deeper below the mountain.

Treasure is what they seek: gold and silver and jewels sleeping beneath the earth. It's not so farfetched to imagine they could become rich as lords overnight.

"Just about makes me feel like an adventurer," someone jokes, and the men all laugh boisterously.

"Hope we don't see no monsters down here."

"It ain't monsters who live this far down. Be more worried about Dark Gods and the like."

Another chorus of laughter. They can't forget the battle five years earlier; the best they can do is laugh it off.

What is life but an accumulation of days, after all? And can you really call it living if you don't enjoy those days?

Maybe you didn't find anything yesterday, but there's always today. If today doesn't work out, there's tomorrow. And then the day after that.

The men knew well that the discovery of a vein of gold demands an accumulation of days.

Furthermore, finding gold is not the end of the matter. Next comes the digging. The delightful work of digging out the gold awaits you.

The miners have no time for gloom; in a way, they bear a burden of their own.

Think about it: without them, the nobles' sparkling jewelry or the coins that change hands in the marketplace wouldn't exist.

We are the ones who support the kingdom. It's an encouraging thought in even the most grueling of endeavors.

There are those working so they can send money home, while others labor to repay the debt for some crime they committed. Others save their money, harboring a foolish dream of becoming adventurers; others still are earning something to support them on the road.

Not that anyone cares a whit about where these people come from or why. The only question is whether they do a good day's work, and they all know it. Be you a criminal or the third son of a noble, in the hole, it doesn't matter, as long as you can dig.

"Right, boys, how about we call it a day?"

"You said it!"

They dig from dawn till dusk, not that one can tell time down below. A great bell booms out from above; that's how they know it's the end of the workday.

There's a general hubbub as everyone works their way out of the mine, tools laid across shoulders.

"Hrm?" one miner mutters, his pickax dug into the face of the wall.

"Somethin' the matter?"

"Wait up. It's stuck on something..."

He pulls as hard as he can. When he frees the ax, however, the end is missing.

In its place is a viscous black ooze, one thread of it still hanging down to the earth.

The miner looks at it vacantly. An instant later, the black goop explodes.

It covers the miner from head to toe; he struggles but can say nothing as it suffocates him.

"Ngah! Wh-what the—!"

"What happened? What's going on?!"

The shouting attracts other miners who had almost been out of the pit.

Maybe it would have been better if they had kept going and not turned around. Although who knows if that would have been the wiser choice?

The first thing they notice as they get back into the mine is the stomach-turning stench of burning flesh. The black liquid is eating through the covered miner, steaming as it goes. The unfortunate victim literally melts away before their eyes, until he's nothing more than a gleaming skeleton.

"This... This might be a man-eating Blob! I've heard about them!"

"Run! It's dangerous!"

Some of the men cling to their pickaxes, the source of their livelihoods, as they flee; others simply cast them aside.

The black goop keeps bubbling up out of the ground, crawling after them.

How many will it claim before they reach the surface...?

The dice of Fate and Chance are utterly without mercy.

CHAPTER 2

Shopping Expedition

Getting Equipment

She could still remember clearly why they had fought.

They must have been about eight years old.

She had been invited to come help with the cows on her uncle's farm, as the animals were about to give birth. Looking back now, she knew that it was just an excuse to give his niece a chance to enjoy herself, but at the time, she had been totally unaware of that.

She would go to town, get a job, and get to ride in a carriage all by herself. She was overflowing with joy and excitement. She felt like she had suddenly become a real grown-up. Now she knew how foolish that was.

She remembered bragging to him: "Pretty cool, huh! You've never even been to town, have you?"

The boy lived next door to her and was two years older than her. Maybe that was why her condescending tone rankled him so much.

It was why she couldn't bring herself to simply say, "Want to come with me?" She wanted him to be the one to say he wanted to go so that she could puff out her chest proudly and say, "Sure!"

But he just stood there with his fists clenched, staring at the ground.

The proximate cause of what she said next was very small. He shouted something, then she shouted something back, and the two of them got worked up over it. The fight ended with both of them weeping copiously.

She never was able to make herself apologize to him. The argument went on until his older sister picked him up.

When she got into the carriage the next day, only her parents were there to see her off.

It meant the last thing she had ever seen of him was his back as his sister led him to their house, his hand in hers.

She never saw him again.

It had been five years already.

§

"Er-errgh…"

A rooster crowed in the distance. The morning sun's rays pierced her eyelids mercilessly.

She could hear someone working in the fields; her uncle must already be about his tasks for the day. She stretched out on her straw bed, but she was only delaying the inevitable. At length, she surrendered, crawling out from under the sheets, exposing her naked body to the bracing air.

"Sooo sleepy…"

She hardly felt as if she had slept at all. She arched her back, causing her well-developed body to jiggle. Her chest and her bottom stood out as especially round, almost embarrassingly so. She wondered why she was so much more developed than other girls her age (though admittedly, she knew few of them). Maybe she had just hit her growth spurt.

Her generous figure, however, didn't make her at all happy. She left her long hair to fall over her face as she stuffed herself into her underwear and then her clothing.

She glanced at the window and thought of opening it but stopped. She just didn't feel like it.

When she got to the dining area, she saw a pile of rye bread in a basket on the table. There was a thin, cold soup waiting in the soup pot.

She took a piece of bread, dipped it in the soup, and munched on it, offering up a small prayer of thanks to the gods for her food.

Only after all this did she come outside, where she looked around and quickly spotted her uncle.

"Good morning, Uncle."

"Ah, g'morning!" A smile split her uncle's craggy, sunbaked face, and he stopped working long enough to greet her. He didn't reprimand her for oversleeping. She bit her lip gently.

"Say," her uncle said. He trailed off before coming up with, "When I'm finished here, I've got some deliveries to make—"

Without waiting for him to finish his sentence—*do you want to come?*—she shook her head and said, "No, thanks." She somehow managed a smile and added, "I don't need to go to...to town."

"I see," he murmured, grimacing. She pressed a hand to her chest.

"Sorry to trouble you," her uncle said, "but could you let the cows out? We need them to eat well and fatten up."

"Yeah," she said with a nod, "sure thing."

She went to the barn with her back hunched and her eyes down to let the animals out. She shook the stick in her hand, calling, "Here, cows! Come on!"

The spring sunlight was pleasantly warm, a breeze running through the daisies that bloomed on the hilltop.

Despite the lovely moment, her heart felt heavy and gray.

What an awful dream.

It was already five years ago. Or was it *just* five years ago?

Five years since the farm on the outskirts of town had taken her in. And yet, look at her.

I'm not a very good girl...

Maybe they shouldn't have anything to do with each other anymore. They only brought each other grief. It would be best if she could get him to just leave her alone, but she couldn't abide the thought of letting him raise her without doing anything in return. For that matter, she wouldn't be able to do anything on her own. She let out a deep sigh.

She realized the cows had wandered to the border of the farm while she was lost in these thoughts.

The road to town ran by on the other side of their fence, and some of the passersby traveling on it glanced at her.

"..."

She found herself oddly discomfited; she blushed and tried to shrink into herself.

"*Here, cows!*" she called, trying to ignore the looks others gave her, but her shout came out almost in a whisper.

It's not like I'm doing anything unusual…

She finally managed to calm down a bit, but the confusion of the world carried on.

The migration of those who had been displaced or starved out by the battle with the Dark Gods five years earlier continued even now. Sometimes, it involved boys and girls not so different in age from her. In place of rucksacks, they carried whatever kind of bag they had on hand; some of them wore swords they seemed to have picked up along the way. All of them frowned and hurried along the road with a certain anxiousness.

They're going to go be adventurers.

She knew it at a glance. In her memory, *he* had looked the same way.

Adventurers. A word to make the heart flutter. Those people explored unknown ruins, fought monsters, found treasure, saved princesses, and sometimes even played a part in the fate of the world.

She had heard that it was a party of adventurers who had been responsible for saving the world five years before.

Many dreamed of becoming adventurers when they were recognized as adults at fifteen years old—or whenever they could pass for old enough. Some of them, of course, had lost homes, couldn't learn a trade, or were otherwise left with no other choice. That didn't take the sheen off the idea of an adventurer, though, and she knew that better than anyone.

Besides, who knew? If things had been just a little bit different, it might have been her on that road. Or she might simply have been gone.

Like him.

"Ergh…"

The thought caused a chill to spread from her stomach through the rest of her body.

Shut it out. Forget everything except for what you have to do right now.

The cows. Call Here cows, here cows, *and then get off this road, quickly.* She'd had enough of it.

She looked up to take a count and make sure all the cattle were there.

"Huh...?" She blinked.

It was at that moment that she thought she had seen, mingled in the crowd, a familiar back...

Had she imagined it? She rubbed her eyes with her sleeve.

No. There's no way.

There was no way, but...

"......"

She stood silent, transfixed, unable to move a muscle.

§

"Excuse meee! I'd like to register as an adventurer, please!"

"Certainly, be right with you!"

"Sorry—could you grab three bags of gold coins from the safe?"

"Sure, right away!"

"Make sure you mark down any potions you sell in the register. We have to balance the books tomorrow."

"Oh, of course! I'm on it!"

"The map! Where's the map?"

"It's on top of the— Here, I'll get it!"

"There's a mistake in this paperwork! A *wyrmling* is a baby dragon; a *worm* is just a bug!"

"Whaa?! I'm very sorry!"

It was so busy that her head was spinning. Staff ran to and fro at the front desk of the Adventurers Guild.

I don't remember my training at the capital being quite like this...!

New Staff Member dashed about like a jumping mouse at top speed, tears welling up in her eyes as she faced the paperwork.

Naturally, it was the staff's job to write out the quests brought to the Guild. Any mistake could be a matter of life and death for some adventurer. The Guild's reputation would be shattered.

Newly hatched or not, a dragon was a dragon. To confuse it with an insect was a mistake of the highest order. An adventurer might take up the quest thinking all they had to do was crush some bug, only to find themselves cooked by the creature's fiery breath.

Actually, at this *level, maybe a worm would be even scarier...*

She took a second to cock her head in thought as she wrote furiously, wrapping a band around her belted-back sleeves. She thought she had heard about something called a purple worm that was supposed to be very strong.

Concerned, she took out the Monster Manual and flipped through the pages.

"So a purple worm is threat level twelve. And a newborn green dragon is…four?"

That means I actually made the opposite of the mistake I thought I did.

She had to do this sort of sleuthing for nearly every quest, and it did her no favors as far as keeping up with her work. There was so much to learn, and she had overtime every day. She got home just in time to have a little dinner and then collapse into bed.

She didn't have much time to get ready in the mornings; it was all she could do to slap on a little makeup and braid her hair. She felt a far cry from the urbane and sophisticated women, so lovely and neat, who she had admired.

Just because she was well educated and came from a family of means and reputation didn't mean she had any obligation to become someone's pretty little wife. She understood the importance of making connections with prominent families in the larger world, ensuring that her father's and husband's work went smoothly. But there were others to take care of such duties. She, for one, was going to enter public service!

And look where it got me.

"Oh, here. Do the papers for all these goblin quests, too."

A pile of papers was deposited in front of her with a thump, and she thought she might burst into tears.

I couldn't become anyone's wife even if I wanted to… I don't have the time!

The receptionist at the next desk saw the expression on the girl's face. "Are you okay?" she asked. The new girl was constantly grateful for the kindness of this other woman, who had said she held a priesthood.

"…Yes, I'm just going to…go get some water."

With things as hectic as they were, she didn't even have time to brew the tea she so enjoyed.

She got to her feet unsteadily, then worked her way over to the communal carafe and poured some water into a cup on which she had written her name. The water was tepid but still felt wonderful on her dry throat and lips. New Staff Member drank noisily, then let out a breath, *phew*.

"Oof… My hand is cramping…"

She rubbed her swollen hand reflexively and massaged her bleary eyes.

Goblins again, huh…

Goblins were, needless to say, the weakest of the monsters, the lowest of the NPCs. With roughly the same size, strength, and intelligence as children, they formed groups and lived in caves or ruins, from which they attacked villages and kidnapped women. They could be cowed into following someone stronger than themselves, but at heart they always believed they were the center of the universe, and it gave them great joy to torment those who were weaker than them.

It was extremely typical for two or three goblins to try to steal livestock from a village, say, and for some group of local youngsters to drive them off. Only when things got quite bad would people go to the Guild. And as a rule, there was no end of "quite bad." It was an almost daily occurrence.

There was even a sort of tongue-in-cheek proverb: every time a party of adventurers forms, so does a goblin nest.

She sometimes wondered why the state didn't do something about them, but she was already at the end of her rope, and wondering was the most she could possibly do.

It had been just five years earlier that the army of Chaos commanded by the Demon Lord had assailed the country like a storm. Even now, elements of his vanquished forces were being discovered throughout the land: Dark Elf assassins wandering at will among the shadows of the capital, plotting malice. Evil cultists practicing horrific rituals in the depths of underground ruins, seeking to revive him. Even necromancers in their houses and towers, using the dead for unspeakable experiments.

Chaotic monsters rampaged across every corner of the map as well, doing what they pleased unchecked.

Never mind the people who want to go fight some dragon off in the mountains.

Goblins were among the most numerous monsters, but that didn't change how pitifully weak they were.

"It makes sense that adventurers might want to fight some other monster..."

Even she didn't like goblins, and all she had to deal with was the paperwork connected to them. It couldn't be much more fun, she surmised, to go around killing them.

If she had been told that, from now on, she had to spend all day, every day doing goblin-related paperwork, she would have made a fuss about it.

New Staff Member gave another deep sigh, then got back to the reception desk waiting for her. She would have to get these goblin-slaying quests sorted out so that they could be posted on the board. Just the thought of it made her stomach churn, and tears sprung to her eyes that she had previously tried holding back.

"Ughhh..."

"Hey, cheer up," her colleague said with a smile from the next desk.

"Right..."

"You know, doing your job is a way of serving righteousness. You should look a little more pleased about it!"

Is this her way of comforting me? I'd be happier hearing it from a cleric of the Earth Mother, not the Supreme God, she thought insolently. *Maybe a servant of the Earth Mother wouldn't work me quite so hard...*

"Hey, have you even eaten lunch?"

Even so, she was indescribably grateful for this display of consideration.

New Staff Member shook her head, causing her braids to sway back and forth. "I haven't had time..."

"Oh, just go and eat. Quick, now! You can't work on an empty stomach! Oops, here comes the next person!"

"Great..."

"Don't forget to smile!"

Despite her coworker's urging, New Staff Member just couldn't muster an appetite. She massaged her cheeks, trying to coax them into the smile she seemed to have so much trouble offering. During her training, she had smiled diligently at every adventurer, wished them the best of luck. But in the end...

It's because I got too involved with them.

She had dark memories of the capital, of a time when she had nearly lost her innocence. Or—well, not quite, but to her, it felt like it. After all, he had been much too strong for a young woman to resist. It was nothing short of a miracle that she had gotten out of it.

But still, I can't send them off with a scowl.

Smiling was just part of the job.

She didn't want to leave those accepting assignments with a sour taste in their mouths. Nor did she want them to misunderstand how she felt. But how much smiling was enough, then?

As she took a moment of her precious time attempting to arrange the expression on her face, a silent presence appeared at the desk.

"..."

A boy stood there before her.

"Er—ah," she said, and the smile she had worked so hard to get onto her face abruptly vanished.

He was about fifteen years old—a bit younger than New Staff Member, and only newly an adult. Wherever he had come from, the journey had left him looking bedraggled.

Judging by his appearance, it seemed likely he was there to become an adventurer. But perhaps he had come from some village to file a quest. She couldn't say.

The boy, however, simply stared at New Staff Member, silent. He almost looked like he was glaring at her.

"A-ahem, wh-what do you—? What can I do for you?"

"No," the boy replied, shaking his head. "Are you all right?"

She didn't quite follow his conversation. Flustered, New Staff Member looked to the neighboring desk for help.

"Listen," a man was saying, "can't you lower the reward a little bit? I can't pay this much for guards."

"Unfortunately, the amount is stipulated in our bylaws," her colleague replied. "Perhaps if you took a lower-rank adventurer..."

"I don't want some amateurs or street thugs around my goods. I need people I can trust..."

She appeared to have her hands full; help would not be forthcoming.

New Staff Member had been told that, although it was less common now, there used to be many quest givers who tried to silence quest takers with violence. There were some suspicious characters who had fled the capital among whom such practices, so she heard, were still common. Hence, the work that the receptionists and other employees at the Adventurers Guild did was very important.

A way of serving righteousness. Okay.

She took a deep breath, then somehow managed to work the smile back onto her face.

"Welcome to the Adventurers Guild! What can I do for you today?"

"If you don't mind, then, I'd like to register."

"R-registration, right! Ahem, just fill out this— E-eep!"

She had scrambled through the papers on her desk a little too eagerly, and they went fluttering down to the floor.

Yes, springtime was when the most people registered as adventurers, but that didn't mean they always had the paperwork right on hand.

As New Staff Member rushed to pick up the papers, the boy caught one in his hand.

"Goblins…?" he asked.

"Goblins? Oh…"

She saw that the sheet of paper he had caught was one of the quests she had finally managed to write out. "Yes, it's a…a goblin-slaying quest, but…"

It was a simple one, at least by the standards of what tended to come to the Guild. The kind of quest you could find by the score anywhere on the frontier.

"Goblins?" He seemed fixated on the word. She held out the paper without so much as glancing at the reward or any other information about the quest. "I request to slay goblins, then."

"Er, uh… It'll be dangerous without a party."

The boy paused in thought for a moment, then said, "It's no problem."

New Staff Member quickly searched her memory. She went to open the Monster Manual, which specifically said that even a party alone was not enough. She remembered hearing repeatedly that you needed more than a few people to take on a goblin quest; she had even made a note about it.

And yet, the way to dissuade someone in a situation like this had completely vanished from her mind.

In a slight panic, she flipped the pages of her notebook, then thought to simply show him the page in the manual. Oh, but could he read?

P-please wait just another moment, she nearly said, but instead, at that exact second, there came a cute little *grr* sound. Blushing so hard she thought steam might come out of her ears, she pressed a hand to her stomach, but the sound came again.

"This, ah, um, this is..."

"It involves goblins, doesn't it?"

"Y-yes..."

Did... Did he not hear me?

She was mortally embarrassed by the growling of her stomach, but she decided to focus on the work of getting him registered.

"All right. So can you read and write?"

"I can," he said. "I learned how."

Then he took the Adventure Sheet she held out for him. His letters were crude, but against appearances, he could indeed write.

She had the distinct sense that if she spent too long watching him, her stomach would make another noise, so she quickly stamped the paper.

"Now, where was it?" she muttered, searching the desk and taking out a quill pen. Yet, she couldn't find the all-important rank tag.

"Huh? Um..."

"Here." Her colleague slid her a porcelain tag, almost as if to say, *What are you doing?*

"Thank you very much!" New Staff Member said with a bow of her head, but her coworker waved her off.

Right, now... The rank tag is basically a copy of the Adventurer Sheet...

New Staff Member took down the information as carefully as she could, being sure she got everything. Name, gender, age, class, hair color, eye color, weight, skills...

One in fighter, one in ranger. Along with...

"There, done!" She let out a deep breath and wiped the sweat from her forehead, mentally patting herself on the back. Then she slid the

©Shingo Adachi

tag across the desk to him: a level marker for Porcelain, the tenth and lowest rank.

"It's very important, so please try not to lose it," she said.

"......"

The boy silently accepted the small porcelain chip; he held it in the palm of his hand and stared intently at it.

"U-ummm—?"

"I understand."

Then he nonchalantly stuck the rank tag in his pocket and walked away with a bold stride.

"Sheesh. What a prick."

These words came from the next person in line, a young man carrying a wooden stick that seemed to be a spear. A few of the other adventurers, new and old alike, glanced after the boy, who had gone in the direction of the workshop.

New Staff Member wasn't sure exactly what to say, but work was work. She refocused herself.

"Welcome to the Adventurers Guild! What can I do for you today?"

"Oh, I wanna register, too, please."

"Right away!" She forced herself to smile as brightly as she could.

I need to learn how to smile better, right away.

She was resolved, determined—and apparently not going to get lunch anytime soon.

Come to think of it... When he asked if I was all right...

Had he been referring to lunch?

The thought hardly lasted a moment amid the busy swirl. Her colleague at the next desk was watching New Staff Member throw herself into her work with an exasperated expression.

Later, she would come to intensely regret that she had not been able to help *him* more diligently. But that's a story for another time.

§

"Er, so, I don't suppose you have any legendary swords on hand... Do you?" the young man asked, his eyes sparkling. All he succeeded in doing, though, was giving the workshop boss a splitting headache.

"If I did, d'you think I'd have 'em just lying around in my shop?"

"Of course not. Sure. What about a storied magical blade? Got any of those?"

"You really think you just go to the store and buy those?" The boss rubbed his eyebrows and shook his head slowly. He almost just kicked the boy out but thought better of it. "For one thing, even a simple enchantment adds a zero to the price of any piece of equipment."

"Right, right… In that case, uhhh…"

The young man looked eagerly at the weapons and equipment lining the shelves, the shine in his gaze undiminished. He picked up this and that experimentally.

"Let's start by talking about your budget," the boss said. "I can't sell what you can't buy."

"Oh, y-yeah. Well, here," the young man said, fishing in his pocket and producing a purse. "I want the most powerful weapon I can buy with this."

He wants the most powerful weapon! Of course he does!

The boss, master of the workshop, heaved a sigh. This was a familiar song and dance. Some bright-eyed young person came in, having been raised on stories of adventure and now convinced that they, too, were a hero in waiting. Visitors as thoroughly ignorant as this young man were unusual, but it was only a matter of degree, not kind. They all wanted swords that were too big for them to use, or armor stripped down so far that the only thing it offered was mobility.

The sum total of these kids' knowledge consisted of some mangled ballad they had heard belted out by a drunken barfly in a tavern somewhere. Such songs were all the rage now, and there was nothing he could do about that, but as hardened as he'd become, it still frustrated him.

The boss considered giving the boy a word of advice, but what good would it do?

"Will a sword do for ya?"

"Yeah. I think a sword sounds good."

The boss took the coin purse, resolving to find the earnest young man a suitable weapon.

Should the sword be one-handed, or two? The young man was

dressed in an outfit of relatively thick leather. The boss doubted it was really fit for someone who fought on the front row.

"Don't want a shield, or a helmet?"

"A helmet? Nah. People wouldn't be able to see my face."

The boss could hardly fault someone for wanting glory; he wasn't about to criticize. Adventurers made their living by selling their faces and reputations. What else was there?

I reckon there isn't a man alive who hasn't wished to be a hero at least once.

"I won't argue about the helmet," he said. "But at least take a shield."

"I've never used one..."

"Doesn't matter."

The boy nodded listlessly in the face of the old man's verdict. Well, he didn't have to be enthusiastic. To the extent he listened to anything at all the boss said, there was hope for the kid. Hope, if nothing else.

There were many who came in with beat-up old gear from their country homes or who made all their purchases without listening to a word he said.

And when it came down to it, the old man could say what he liked, but he was not the one who would have to face monsters in battle.

No matter what equipment you carried, you would die when it was your time—so perhaps he should simply let them do whatever they wished. It would be a shame for someone to let him sway their opinion, and then to die wearing equipment they hadn't even wanted.

No matter how stupid, or ugly, or ridiculous the equipment they wanted might have been...

Who could mock any young person for the choices they made while deliberately taking their first steps out into the wider world? When the boss thought back to the very first time in his life that he had taken up a hammer and tried to forge a sword...

"Hmm?"

It was at that moment that another young person came into the workshop from the direction of the Guild reception area, walking boldly yet nonchalantly.

"I need equipment."

"So ya do," the old man said, involuntarily frowning at the curt declaration.

The young man who had been in the middle of shopping pricked up his ears with boyish interest. The boss made a shooing motion at him and turned his attention to the youthful newcomer.

He looks pathetic.

The boy was in sorry shape, as if he had just come fleeing all the way from some far, rustic corner.

"Do ya have coin?"

"Yes," the boy said, then removed a small leather pouch from around his neck and set it on the counter. It jangled as the money inside settled.

The old man prodded open the pouch with one finger, then took out one of the gold coins inside and bit down on it.

It wasn't just leaf. These were the real thing.

The grizzled shopkeeper brushed the flower pattern sewn into the purse, then eyed the boy. "Made off with Mommy's purse, did we? Or perhaps Sister's?"

"..."

For a second, the boy didn't say anything; then he nodded. "That's right."

The shopkeeper gave a dissatisfied snort. Was the kid joking or not?

Either way, this was real gold in front of him, and a customer with cash was a customer he would do business with.

"Right, then. What is it ya want?"

"Tough leather armor and a round shield."

"Oh-ho," the old man breathed. He took a fresh look at the boy, ignoring the dumbfounded expression on his previous customer's face.

Well muscled. Clearly a fighter. Probably multi-classed, maybe as a scout or a ranger. Neither would be unusual.

"And for a weapon?"

"A sword... One-handed."

"Obviously, given the shield. I think this is the one for you." Without pausing, the old man grabbed one of the blades lined up behind the counter and handed it over. It was a steel sword. There was nothing especially unique about it, but it was a perfectly sturdy, serviceable weapon.

The boy took it and put it in a sheath at his side. The weight caused him to lean slightly.

Common enough with greenhorns.

"The leather armor is on the shelf back there. Shields are on the wall."

"All right."

The boy forcefully corrected the lean, then marched over to where the old man had indicated. The furtive way in which he took some armor from the table and a shield from the wall made it look almost as if he were stealing them. The old man allowed himself to look nearly impressed for a moment. Suddenly, the other young new adventurer, who had seemed so cowed, moved.

"H-hey," he said, "did you just register today?"

The boy didn't answer out loud but nodded his head.

That prompted the young man to smile and say, "Me too!" He puffed out his chest. "H-hey, how about you and I go on an adventure together?"

"An adventure," the boy echoed softly. The young man's voice seemed to fly excitedly in the sky, while the boy's veritably crawled on the ground. "Does it involve goblins?" His voice was brusque.

"Hardly!" the young man exclaimed. His whole body seemed to shake with the eagerness to deny the idea. "I'm aiming a little higher than that. Forget goblins. I'm thinking unknown ruins and stuff..."

"I want goblins."

"Huh?"

"I'm gonna go slay goblins."

With that, the boy seemed to lose interest in the young man. He put on the armor with an unpracticed but relatively quick hand, then strapped the shield to his arm. It was small and round, and in addition to the strap, it had a handle. He grabbed it and took some gentle practice blocks.

He stood with the shield at the ready, drew his sword, then sheathed it again. He tried moving a bit, then nodded.

"I'll take them."

"Pleasure."

"How much do I have left?"

"About this much," the old man said, pouring the contents of the purse onto the counter. He collected a dozen or so of the gold coins and swept them behind the counter.

Now only a few were left. The young man muttered, "Rip-off," earning a glare from the shopkeeper.

"Preparing hard leather takes time. It's not cheap," he said. "If you don't like it, shop somewhere else." The old man would not commit the folly of skimping on the work of padding the leather after he had boiled it in oil.

The boy, for his part, seemed unmoved by the comment; he touched each gold coin, counting them up.

"Can I buy a potion?"

"Next time you want one, get it at the reception desk. Not that I don't have some here..."

He accepted more money from the boy, exchanging it for two bottles he pulled out from behind the counter. A light-green liquid rippled gently inside them, and they smelled faintly of medicine.

"An antidote and a healing potion. Good enough?"

"Yes," the boy said and put both bottles into his item bag.

There was one coin left.

"Is there anything else I should have?"

"Hmm, let's see, now... An Adventurer's Toolkit, a dagger..."

The old man looked the boy over from head to toe. He was clad in leather armor, a sword in one hand and a shield in the other. Combined with his bag full of miscellaneous items, he looked every inch the novice adventurer.

"If you ask me...maybe a helmet."

"A helmet."

"Wait right there. I've a cheap one."

The boss walked back into the workshop's storeroom. The young man, already done with his shopping, looked at the boy dubiously. He seemed to be thinking, in a word, *What's with this guy?* or perhaps more accurately, *What a weirdo.*

Finally, the young man shook his head and muttered, "Makes no sense to me," and showed himself out of the workshop.

At almost the same moment, the old boss emerged from the storeroom.

"I'd suggest you wear one of these," he said. "If you're not too worried about whether people can see your face."

Then he placed the helmet he was holding on the counter.

It was old, with horns growing out of either side. A devilish-looking thing indeed.

§

The Adventurers Guild is busy as ever with comings and goings. How much does any one adventurer stand out in that crowd? His armor is brand-new, unblemished. He has a horned steel helmet. At his hip is a sword, and on his arm is a newly bought shield.

What else can we call the young man in this gear but a novice adventurer?

When he walks out the door and into town, nobody notices.

Nobody would notice, either, if he never came back.

Nobody at all.

INTERLUDE

Of Their First Time

"Awesome! Let's get started..."

The mouth of the cave yawned wide enough to swallow the trees all around. The heavy warrior tried to sound as ready and impressive as he could.

It was just a simple quest—or it was supposed to be.

Goblin slaying. A bog-standard hack and slash.

Allegedly, the goblins had built a nest near a village and begun stealing livestock and the like. At some point, they would presumably move on to people. The villagers wanted someone to get rid of the goblins before it was too late. It was a perfectly typical story.

He remembered once in his own village—in his own youth—when some adventurers had come. In his memory, they seemed amazing, larger than life, and so sure of themselves. But as for him...

Guess I've got a long way to go.

Heavy Warrior's hands opened and closed of their own accord. He tried to get the still-unfamiliar gauntlets to feel right.

What was he so worried about? Every adventurer started out with this kind of quest, didn't they? It was nothing to be afraid of.

Or was it...?

What if—just on the off chance—he was defeated and had to go crawling back home? He would have to go limping back to the village he had left so dramatically just weeks before.

And that's the last thing I want…!

It wasn't just about looking bad. The big thing was his best buddy had stolen the girl he liked.

Well, it had been more of a crush on his part. He hadn't even told her he liked her…he thought. So maybe that didn't count as having her stolen? He didn't know, but it didn't matter. He didn't want to come between them, and neither did he want to go home with his tail between his legs.

Hell, I chased goblins off from our village.

So he was sure…well, fairly sure…that assuming nothing out of the ordinary happened, he would be all right. And he wasn't alone.

Come to think of it, the adventurers who came to our village had a party, too.

As the thought crossed his mind, Heavy Warrior stopped where he was in the bushes.

"What? What's wrong? Why'd you stop? If you're stopping, let me take point." Beside him, Female Knight smiled eagerly, like a mischievous child. The fact that she already had her sword out and ready spoke both to her savagery and her eagerness for combat.

She was just grumbling over her drink when I found her at the tavern. Maybe I was wrong to talk her into joining my group.

"It's nothing," he said. "Just got lost in thought for a moment."

He shook his head to clear the doubt from his mind. He was his party's leader, as far as it went (and it didn't go very far). There was a lot he had to do.

Heavy Warrior thought desperately back to how the older men of his village had acted when he was helping in the fields.

"Come on, kid—er, the one who can use all the magic…"

"Don't you think it's about time you remembered my name?" Druid Girl groused, puffing her cheeks out in a way that made her look more cute than angry.

Beside her, Scout Boy had his knife in his hand and was eyeing the cave warily. As far as outfits, both of them managed to look like adventurers—poor ones.

They're more childish than I really expected…

He had been forced to recruit a magic user and a scout with only the knowledge he had gleaned from the songs of bards, and this was the result:

a couple of kids who had lied about their ages in order to become adventurers. At the moment, however, he had no choice but to rely on them.

I probably can't ask too much of them, but...it is what it is.

"Save your magic," he said. "We don't know what's in there."

That was the unvarnished truth.

It wasn't as if he expected to run into a dragon—a creature he had no intention whatsoever of disturbing—but anything and everything was possible. There was a famous parable about someone who was walking down the street when they had a random encounter with a drake.

Still, the order made Heavy Warrior feel a bit too much like his own fear was showing, so he tried to add a word of encouragement.

"Don't use your magic if you don't need to," he said.

"Y-yeah, sure," Druid Girl said, her head bobbing up and down and her hands on her staff.

"So," Heavy Warrior said, looking at Scout Boy, who hardly seemed to blink. "Hey."

"R-right!" The boy jumped a little and replied in a scratchy voice.

How am I supposed to handle moments like this?

Heavy Warrior tried hard to think back to when the goblins had come to his village.

"Breathe deeply," he instructed. "In, out, until I say to stop."

"S-sure thing!" The boy nodded vigorously; it was hard to say whether it had helped. But at least Heavy Warrior had gotten him to make the effort to calm down. That would have to do for now.

But wasn't there...something else?

Something you were supposed to do right before an adventure, right before you went slaying goblins.

Wasn't there something else that had to be done? Had to be taken care of? Seen to?

Heavy Warrior found himself frowning, assaulted by an unidentifiable anxiety. He turned to his half-elf fighter.

"Hey, am I missing anything?"

"Let's see," Half-Elf Fighter said in what seemed like a thoughtful tone. He turned his head gracefully, taking in each of the members of the party, then clapped his hands and said lightly, "Ah! Let's set up our formation first. 'We don't know what's in there,' right?"

"Our formation?"

As in, the scout would be out front, ahead of the party, while the spell casters stayed in the back row. Did he mean like that?

As Heavy Warrior struggled to put his all too modest knowledge into practice, Female Knight tapped him on the shoulder.

"Just so you know, I have a healing miracle!"

Why was she saying that here and now? What purpose would it serve?

Heavy Warrior looked away from Female Knight, who was triumphantly puffing out her chest in a most unladylike fashion. He sighed.

They had the potions they had all gone in together to buy. Why should they need to go begging the gods for—

No. Remember… We really don't *know what's in there.*

"Even if we don't need it this time, who can say about next time? Great, fine, good."

Good indeed. He resolved to be grateful for every card he was granted to play.

Then Heavy Warrior glanced at Druid Girl and sighed for the umpteenth time. She was standing there, muttering her incantation to herself in hopes that she would remember it. Not a sight that inspired confidence. Given the way she looked like a child on her first trip out of town, he didn't think he was wrong to wonder about her. Left to the tail of the group, she looked like she might get lost or simply fall down.

Maybe we should put one of our front-row people at the back.

"Okay, O miracle-wielding knight. You're the caboose. I'm trusting you to bring up the rear."

"Right! Leave it to me!" The way she pounded the chest plate of her armor really communicated nothing but fear—but so be it.

He had done everything he could think of. The thought helped Heavy Warrior relax a little.

"Okay, shall we get going?"

He pounded Scout Boy on the back, then hefted his broadsword and started off.

About fifteen minutes later, he would find himself in trouble when the sword started getting caught on every wall.

CHAPTER 3

TUTORIAL

First Adventure

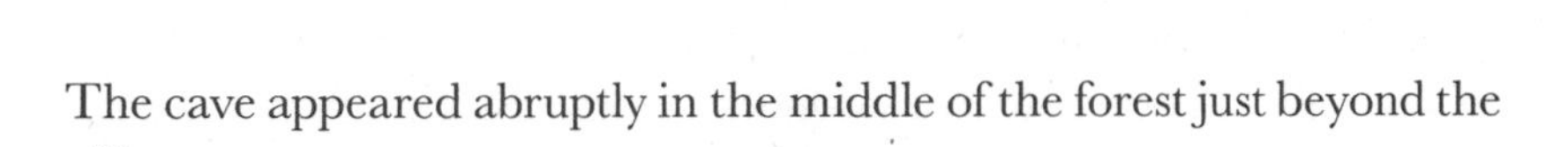

The cave appeared abruptly in the middle of the forest just beyond the village.

How long had it been there? None of the villagers remembered.

It seemed as though it had been there forever—and yet, at the same time, it was like the cave had only just recently come to be, in a flash. Such an impression was common here on the frontier, which had not been under human development for very long.

Every part of the world was continually changing. Even among the elves there was none who knew the exact geography of all places.

And now, goblins had made a home in this cave. Were they stragglers, survivors from the battle five years earlier? Or just wild creatures? Nobody knew.

What people did know was that goblins had appeared out of that cave, attacked the village, stolen some livestock, and finally, kidnapped a woman.

A common tale, he thought.

Including the part where someone came to the Adventurers Guild to file a quest.

Now, he faced the mouth of the cave, hiding himself in the forest undergrowth, waiting intently for time to go by. The sun had passed its zenith and was working its way down through the sky. He spent the hours before twilight in observation.

The goblins went in and out of their nest, showing no sign of noticing him. The guards didn't take their jobs seriously, standing around almost, it seemed, out of habit.

What drew his attention was the strange tower that stood just beside the pile of waste near the entrance.

It doesn't appear to be any kind of trap.

The goblins he saw coming and going carried weapons, among other things. He just watched them and tried to breathe as quietly as possible. He remembered his sister telling him that this was a necessary skill for a hunter. Deer were skittish animals; if they didn't think you were part of nature, they would run away.

His father, so he gathered, had been quite good at this, although he'd never gotten the chance to see it himself.

At last, the sun began to sink in the west, and the sky turned an eerie purple color. For some reason, the guards had disappeared from the mouth of the cave. They must have gone back inside.

It's time.

He stood slowly from the bushes, first massaging his stiff joints. He had hoped the walk from town would be enough to accustom himself to his first set of armor, but there was no denying it was a bit heavy. What was more, simply lying in wait all day was enough to stiffen the body.

Maybe I'll loosen the straps of my equipment while resting.

Once he had sufficiently relaxed his joints, he checked over his equipment. He raised and lowered the visor on his helmet, drew and sheathed his sword, made sure the blade was still sharp.

The horns on the helmet made his head especially heavy. His field of vision was narrow, and he found it difficult to breathe. But he didn't have the courage to take it off.

He grasped the handle of the shield strapped to his arm, making some experimental feints. No problems.

He stepped out of the bushes, careful not to rustle them, and slowly approached the cave entrance. He didn't walk with his usual bold stride but, instead, moved delicately.

He passed by the weird tower topped with an animal skull, then stopped next to the pile of waste.

Should he light the torch or not? And was there anything else he had forgotten?

A light source would give away his position to anyone with line of sight. And yet, the enemy could see in the dark and would find him first even without a torch. In such circumstances, having no light could only be considered a disadvantage.

He took a torch from his item bag and made to strike a flint to it but then stopped.

"..."

He was just realizing something that should have occurred to him earlier.

I can't hold a torch like this.

He had a sword in his right hand and a shield in his left. It was inconceivable that he would go without his blade, yet neither did he want to give up his only defense. He tried letting go of the shield's grip in order to hold the torch, but the exaggerated angle of his wrist made it hard to move his arm.

He let out a very frustrated groan, cursing his own stupidity and foolishness. If his master had been watching, he would never have lived this down.

He spent a while in thought, looking into the cave entrance, and then gave up. Torch in the right hand, shield in the left, sword at his hip, and bag on his back. What was a torch but a wooden stick? It could double as a club if need be.

He resolved to have the handle of his shield removed when he got back to town, then advanced into the entrance.

Of course, he acknowledged, *that's* if *I get back to town.*

§

"Surely you don't think you're lucky just because I'm teaching you? That you're blessed?"

He was fairly sure those were the words the old rhea man had said as he had kicked the boy into the ice cave.

The boy tumbled into the cave, which was full of waste and old food, the most disgusting place he had ever been.

Rhea dwellings were renowned as some of the most comfortable, pleasant places in the world. That, at least, was what he heard later.

The rheas were supposedly a people who lived among the fields, enjoying their daily labors and a distinct lack of adventure. They were cheerful and easygoing, given to a certain impulsiveness.

Well, there are exceptions to every rule—and the old rhea man was the exception to this one.

The rhea ignored the boy's fit of coughing and closed the wooden door to the cave, barring it.

"The really lucky ones are the ones who can do anything without needing to be taught."

There were no lights where the boy was, so he was plunged instantly into darkness. When he finally steadied his breath and looked around himself, he could see nothing at all.

Nothing except a pair of eyes glimmering in the shadows: the old rhea.

He realized they were focused directly on him, and he gulped.

"You're not that type, though. You can't do a thing. Incompetent, shit-eating kid."

"Yes, Master," the boy finally managed. Strangely, he didn't think he was going to be killed.

Of killing and being killed, he had learned more than his share at his village.

But he suspected the old man could murder without giving it a thought.

"You think if I teach you, you'll get stronger," the rhea sneered.

Before the boy could so much as utter a *yes*, something came flying through the darkness and struck him in the forehead. It broke with a crackling sound, a warm pain running through the boy's skull. Blood dribbled down his face.

He stumbled. The rhea kicked him down, then loomed over him tauntingly.

"Damn fool. As if an insect with a weapon were anything but an insect."

It was a plate, the boy realized. He'd been hit with a plate.

He had never known such a simple thing could hurt so much.

"Use everything you have. Prepare your equipment. If there's something you want, and you don't do everything in your power to get it..."

Now that he thought about it, that may have been the first lesson his teacher ever imparted to him.

"...then what's the point of even being alive?"

§

An acrid smell hit his nostrils the moment he entered the cave.

Rotten garbage. Filth. Bodily waste. The lingering stench of carnality.

He was used to it all. They wouldn't be a serious problem for him.

The darkness, however, was proving an obstacle. He had a torch, yes, but the blackness was overpowering. His mind filled with thoughts of what might be hiding in the flickering shadows at the edge of his torchlight.

Not might be...*what* is *hiding.*

There was no room to doubt that fact. He must not forget where he was: in a goblin den.

If I force myself to breathe through my nose, I'll get used to the smell. Human senses are convenient that way.

He stood still and steadied his breath, then slid one foot forward, beginning his advance. It would be all too easy to lose his footing on the wet earth and the moss that covered the stone. He tried to focus on his steps, but the darkness quickly began to bother him.

What awaited him ahead? Or above? The cave itself seemed to close in on him. His breathing became shallower, more rapid. Trying to pay attention to everything at once was making him dizzy.

"...Take one thing at a time," he murmured to himself, then turned his torch on the shadow of a rock wall.

He just needed to take them down steadily. Don't begrudge the time and effort to make your own life easier—that was what his master would have said.

He tried to control his breathing as he listened to his surroundings, hoping not to miss anything. Besides the ragged sound of his own inhale and exhale, he detected a faint ringing in his ears. He didn't know if it was because of the silence or borne of his nervousness.

He wanted to take off his helmet and wipe the sweat from his brow. But of course, he couldn't do that. He blinked repeatedly, then suddenly stared into the dark.

Maybe it was his imagination. Then again, maybe not.

He reflexively threw his torch at the wriggling shadow, right at the place that had moved differently from the rest of the darkness.

"GOOROB?!"

A scream went up, a choked cry. It was still alive. He leaped at it and pounded another blow between its eyes. He felt an unpleasant mushiness, like smashing a fruit, as the goblin expired and its brains went flying.

"...Nghaa."

He let out a quick, loud breath. At the same moment, he thought he might fall over, the strength going out of his legs.

He realized the spray of blood had nearly put out the half-broken torch. He thought it might be best to throw it away, but somehow he couldn't let it go. His hand simply wouldn't open.

His hand and fingers shook; no matter what he did, he couldn't seem to let the tension out of them.

"..."

He gave a single annoyed click of his tongue, then forced the fingers of his left hand open, dropping the torch. The guttering flame rolled on the floor of the cave but continued to burn, licking the air like a tongue.

It was nothing. Nothing, he told himself. What did it mean to kill a goblin?

One goblin. Still just one. Only one. But he had managed to kill it. He checked again to be sure it was dead, then reached for another torch—

"GOBGG!"

"GBBGROBG!"

He abandoned the torch and drew his sword instead. The next instant, innumerable gibbering goblins came flying at him from behind.

He tried to spin and sweep them away with his sword, but the blade was knocked from his hand with a sickening clatter. Even as he registered that it had caught against the wall, a goblin was ramming into him, knocking him down. His item pack made a loud clang behind him as he landed, but he had no time to take note of it.

"GROB! GOOROGB!!"

"GROORB!!"

One goblin, a hideous smile on its face, slashed at him with a dagger it held in both hands. The torch, nearly extinguished on the ground, still produced enough light to make the blade glitter dimly. Farther away, another goblin was pointing at him and smiling wickedly.

I'm going to die.

"Hrr—agh!"

By sheer force of will, he bent his left arm, bringing his shield up in front of his face. The dagger lodged in the shield, and he swung it outward.

"GBBROB?!"

Goblins are not physically strong. With the weapon ripped from its grasp, the creature was thrown off balance.

He immediately arched his back, pushing his abdomen up and forcing the goblin backward. There was no time to waste. If a larger group showed up now, he would be mincemeat.

The goblin he had knocked to the ground was now trying to scramble to its feet, but he wasn't about to give it the chance.

"?!"

The creature gave a breathless gasp as he kicked it in the stomach with the reinforced toe of his boot, the force tearing open its abdomen and spilling viscera onto the ground. Then he brought his foot down, with a motion as if he were shaking off dirt, and crushed its groin.

"GBORROGBGOR?!"

"GROB! GROORBG!!"

His victim screamed piteously, while the other goblin cackled at his companion's misfortune.

The laughter didn't last long.

The boy was already picking up the sword he had lost, ramming it mercilessly into the goblin's throat. The creature coughed, choking on its own blood; it tried to hold on to the blade. He kicked it away, drawing out his sword.

"Huff..."

Blood gushed all around him. He was hot all over, breath ragged, a dull aching in his head. His throat tickled; he wanted nothing more than to take a swig from his canteen. But there wasn't time.

He could feel something creeping nearby. There was a scratching noise coming from behind him in the dark.

He groaned softly and gritted his teeth. At the same time, he tried to think. He must not stop thinking.

It was obvious that there must have been an ambush tunnel behind him. He had simply missed it. The question was, how had his entry been noticed? He had gone in when there were no guards, and the first goblin hadn't made too much noise.

"...!"

Then, he had a flash of insight and looked down at his gear. It was brand-new, gleaming, untarnished. Leather and steel.

The smell!

He was late realizing it. The goblins were nearly upon him. He checked his sword. It was still fairly free of blood and guts, but the blade had a large chip in the middle. He clicked his tongue.

He plunged his hand into his item bag, where he thought he felt something strange. Nonetheless, he grabbed the torch and threw it to the ground. It caught the flame of the guttering torch, flaring up in a burst of light. The illumination reflected countless yellow eyes shimmering with hatred and murder.

"GOOROGB!"

"GROB! GOBORB!!"

"GOOROGBGROOB!!"

Then he was swept up in chaos.

He crouched down, keeping his back to the wall and raising his shield. He thrust out with his sword, trusting to luck to land any blows.

He didn't want to make the same mistake he had before. He focused on stabbing the goblins. This way would work.

Throat, eyes, stomach, heart. He lashed out with the sword, piercing through, seeking places that would kill in a single blow.

But he and the goblins were equally intent on killing one another. Rusty daggers and spears struck his exposed arms and legs, tearing at them, drawing blood. The goblins, however, started getting in one another's way, tripping over one another and jabbing elbows into their brethren; a series of ugly arguments started. Goblins hardly knew the word *teamwork*.

At the moment, all he needed to do was to keep stabbing with his sword. Everything that wasn't him was an enemy. That made things easy.

So he gritted his teeth and kept working. If his arm gave out, he would surely die; that was all there was to it.

Blood and fat, flesh and bone: he resented the blade for growing duller each time he used it. Perhaps it would have been different if he were a more accomplished fighter.

Then came a great *thud* that heralded a change in the tide of battle.

Beyond the immediate horde, there was a large—massive, really—goblin shuffling toward the fray. A club rested across its shoulders, and it plodded like a man on his way to work the fields.

"HOOOOB..."

It almost looks like a hob, he thought, his breath coming in gasps. A hob: a hobgoblin. Was there any chance of victory? Yes.

His body moved mechanically. It was just like tossing a silver ball into the mouth of a frog. The sword rotated in his hand until he was holding it in a reverse grip. Simultaneously, he slammed the goblin in front of him with his shield, killing it. His master had taught him that if you crush someone's nose and keep pushing, it will go back into their brain and kill them.

Now he swept with his sword, taking his first step away from the rock face.

Throw.

"GOROOGB?!"

A critical hit.

The sword whistled through the air, passing easily over the heads of the goblins and lodging itself in the hobgoblin's throat. Clawing at the empty air, the creature toppled over, slamming into the ground. Pathetic.

He grabbed the dagger at his waist, turning his attention to the remaining enemies.

"GROBG?!"

"GRG! GOOROGGB!!"

The surviving clutch of goblins were looking in every direction.

They stared dumbly at their bodyguard's corpse, then looked at the boy in front of them with his armor and his mask, and promptly ran screaming in the other direction.

They dropped their weapons as they fled into the cave, but he didn't have the wherewithal to chase them now. Dragging his battered, bleeding body forward, he bore down on the still-twitching hobgoblin.

"Take…this!"

With both hands, he grabbed the sword that was still lodged in the creature's neck and tore out its windpipe with all his strength. There was a cracking sound, and the blade split in two at the nick he had noticed earlier.

The boy lost his balance, slipping in a pool of blood. Suddenly, he desperately wanted lemonade.

In his hands, he found himself holding a haft and about two-thirds of a sword. He got unsteadily to his feet and gave it an experimental swing; he found it unexpectedly nimble.

This is good.

At last, he was able to breathe again; he looked around himself.

"How many was that…?"

It was carnage. There was no other term for the picture illuminated by the lolling torch.

Now that the stomach-turning fight was over, he began to trample on the dead goblins' corpses.

How many had he killed? How many had fled? And how many were left? He had no idea.

How many goblins were even in this cave to start with?

"…"

As the thought sank in, he shook his heavy head slowly from side to side.

Whatever the case, it was clear what he should do—what he *had* to do.

"Guess I'll start with first aid."

He reached into the bag of items on his back. Needless to say, he was exhausted. His breath was harsh, his pulse flying and his vision blurry. His nerves were giving out, and the rush of blood dulled his thoughts something terrible.

That was why he didn't notice it.

"GOGGBR!!"

The boy cried out.

The goblin with the crushed groin jumped at him, brandishing a dagger. By the time he felt something heavy collide with his back, it was too late. He tried to turn around, only for his head to suffer a violent jerk. The monster must have grabbed on to one of the horns.

"Hrr... Why, you...!"

"GBGGB!"

He almost thought his right shoulder had exploded. It took him several seconds to register that the goblins had stabbed him with the dagger.

He was coughing up blood in time with his pulse, spattering his helmet.

"Grraaaahhh...!" he growled, trying to fall backward toward the wall. He slammed into the rock.

There was a scream: "GOOROG?!"

Again.

"GORO?!"

Once more.

"GOROOBGBG?!"

There was a dry crack, and suddenly, the weight on his head and back was lifted. Even so, his head hung at a terrible angle. The horn must've broken off.

He turned around, using his still-functioning left hand to grab the horn off the ground. He ended up hurting his wrist, because the shield was still attached. But he didn't care. He had one thing to do.

He slammed into the monster writhing on the ground, shoving the horn through its throat.

"GOOBGGB...?!"

The goblin howled, then ceased moving. The boy just managed to sit down—rather than collapsing—next to it.

First aid. That was what mattered. Healing. There were still enemies about. He couldn't let himself be rendered immobile.

"Hrgh..."

But his whole body shook. He thought wounds were supposed to burn, yet he felt terribly cold.

He made to remove the dagger with his left hand, but his arm twitched and his mouth slackened; drool ran from his lips.

He soon understood why.

He drew the dagger out forcefully to discover a viscous, unidentifiable liquid coating it.

"Hrr…kk…"

Poison.

He tossed the dagger aside and it clattered to the ground.

He plunged his hand into his item bag again. He had bought an antidote. This would be all right. He would be all right…

"…Hrk…?"

All he could feel against his fingers, though, was a wet sensation, and tinkling bits of something like glass.

But there were no bottles.

They broke…!

He felt himself going pale, and it wasn't just because of the poison.

It must have broken when he had fallen in the ambush earlier. Well, regret would do nothing for him now.

If he got back to town—no, to the village—could they help him? It was impossible. His body would barely listen to him; he felt as weak as if he were ridden with fever.

If this went on, he was going to die. There was no question.

Silently, he pulled the bag close with a trembling hand. He pushed the edge of the bag through his visor and wrung it out.

A mixture of healing and antidote potions dribbled into his mouth; he suckled at it desperately, like a tender child at his mother's breast.

He had no intention whatsoever of dying.

At least, not today.

§

The chieftain grumbled angrily as he was interrupted by one of his lackeys, pale-faced, crying, *Intruder! Intruder! Intruder!*

He gave the underling a smack with his staff and kicked his now-silent goblin-mother. "Tell me," he demanded.

He quickly pieced together the lackey's confused account. He was smart that way.

It seemed an adventurer had entered the nest—and all alone, at that.

What a fool. The chieftain laughed. He would soon die in an ambush. It was a shame that the newcomer was a man, but males were still useful for their meat. It was really no bad thing.

That was what the chieftain thought—but he was wrong.

Not only had the adventurer thwarted the sneak attack, but he had even killed their Wanderer.

The chieftain rained foul curses upon the adventurer, stamping the ground in frustration; he gave the lackey another whack for good measure.

He wasn't specifically angry that his minions had been killed. But he couldn't stand the thought of his perfect (in his eyes) nest being upset by this intruder.

Get together whoever's still alive, he growled, and the goblin who had fled to him now went running off again, howling.

Curse and ruin these damnable adventurers. Making me have to go grab myself another goblin-mother.

It suited goblins to believe that because they were weak, they were always the victims. Yet, in their hearts of hearts, they saw themselves as the most important creatures in the world, and that was what made them so profoundly unpleasant.

The chieftain put the spurs to the four goblins who had come back alive as he sought battle with the adventurer. He would finish the job himself. His followers wouldn't settle for anything less. After all, half the reason a goblin nest's existence continued at all was the leader's untrusting nature; the other half was the jealousy of his followers.

If he wasn't careful, the idiots who surrounded him might get in his way. And that, the chieftain couldn't abide.

Luckily for him, it was reported that the adventurer had been wounded in combat. There was a stippled trail of blood leading toward the entrance, away from the piles of corpses of his moronic fellows. What was more, the footprints suggested the adventurer had been all but dragging himself along. He was badly wounded, no question about it.

The chieftain smiled wickedly; he gestured with his staff to encourage the others. Arguing and complaining, they moved forward, until at last they arrived at the mouth of the cave. The great hole let in the light of the green moon, the whole place filling with the brightness of "morning."

There was no way the adventurer would escape under these conditions. The chieftain waved his staff, sending his fellow goblins out of the cave.

The moment he did so, there was a wet *smack*, and two of the goblins were simply obliterated.

"GOROB?!"

What had happened? The chieftain wasn't sure at first, but he thought something large had fallen down from above.

It was the hobgoblin's corpse. As far as the chieftain was concerned, the huge lug was a worthless lump of waste that was still causing problems for him even after it was dead.

It had never occurred to the chieftain that the adventurer might drag the corpse up somewhere and then push it down on the goblins.

"GOBBBR!"

"GBO! GROOBGR!!"

The remaining two goblins, having narrowly avoided disaster, turned to the chieftain with fear on their faces.

Accursed, brainless fools. The chieftain gave them each a smack on the noggin and kicked them out of the cave.

Immediately, something fell down and attacked one of them.

This something was an adventurer, wearing armor and a helmet. The horn on one side of his helmet was broken off.

"GORB?!"

The adventurer started by slamming his shield into the head of the nearest goblin, splitting the creature's face open.

"GOROBRG?!"

Then he spun, catching the second goblin (who had snuck up behind him) with the edge of the shield in a sideward sweep. The metal edge wasn't sharp enough to be called a blade, but it was plenty to shatter the creature's chest, causing it to let out a scream.

The adventurer clicked his tongue when he realized he had failed to finish the monster in a single blow, then jumped upon it, slamming the shield into its throat. Windpipe crushed, the goblin suffocated over the next several seconds.

For the chieftain, it was enough.

They might be stupid piles of excrement, but they had at least served to buy him time to incant his spell.

The chieftain was already raising his staff, topped with an animal's skull, and declaiming an incomprehensible curse.

The adventurer realized what he was doing and turned, but it was too late.

At that instant, lightning burst forth from the staff.

§

It was a Thunderbolt.

He had not realized such things existed: goblins who could use magic.

He braced himself with his right arm—he wasn't about to sacrifice his good left arm—and used the hobgoblin's body to shield himself. Blue-white lightning slammed into the corpse, crackling and fizzing as it burned his arm.

He didn't cry out—on some level, he didn't experience it as pain, but rather a loss of sensation, almost like his arm had been flung through the air.

"Argh...!"

In fact, he had been thrown several feet from the hobgoblin's body. A weird, medicinal flavor spread through his mouth, and sweat suddenly dripped from every pore.

He rolled along the ground, then used his left hand to push himself to his feet.

What about the right?

He looked down and saw his arm. He wouldn't have believed it if he hadn't seen it, but it was still attached. He tried to move it, but it didn't quite respond the way he expected, almost as if it were badly swollen.

It was not, however, without sensation.

The pain was difficult to describe: it was as if instead of an actual arm, he had a thousand needles that happened to look like one.

And there was more. He clicked his tongue. The goblin in front of him was raising its staff again.

He would figure out what this creature was later. If his right arm was still there at the end of the fight, he would deal with that then, too. He had to kill the monster before another bolt came.

The hobgoblin's body twitched with the last of the electricity, smoke rising from the cooked flesh. The corpse had given him some cover but hadn't protected him entirely. That much was obvious now.

What could he do, then? What equipment did he have on hand? What options were available to him? And what path should he take?

How can I kill this creature?

His mind worked quickly, reviewing the possibilities. He undid the strap on the back of his shield, gripping it by the handle.

"GOOBOOGOROGOBOG!!"

The chieftain—the goblin shaman—bellowed the words of the spell again, and a second Thunderbolt rent the air. Its blue-white light bent at wild angles but came flying straight at him.

"—ngh!"

He caught the assault on his shield—the shield he had thrown with his left hand from the shadow of the hobgoblin's corpse.

It flew in a sharp arc, intercepting the lightning and sending it flying off in another direction.

Easier than throwing silver balls into the mouths of frogs at a festival.

The bright light filled his vision, and the acrid smell of scorched leather reached his nose; black smoke billowed into the air. The situation wasn't conducive to seeing well at all. The flash was still imprinted on his retinas. But the same would be true of his enemy.

And that's good enough.

He took his sword, now of a strange length, in his left hand. He raised it in a reverse grip and jumped through the smoke to attack the shaman.

"Ha—ahh!"

"GBBRGGGG!"

The shaman thrust its staff upward. Could it use yet another spell? He didn't know, but it didn't matter.

What I must do is simple.

He jumped, clearing the hobgoblin's body, staying as low as he could, bringing his sword up, then down toward the throat.

That was all.

"GOBORG?!"

There was an impact hard enough to knock someone down; he felt something under him, heard the scream and saw the spray of blood. It seemed even the broken blade of the sword was enough to destroy a goblin throat.

That should keep it from being able to use any more spells.

Even as the foul goblin gore drenched him, he leaned in with his weight, hoping to break its bones. It was more difficult than he had hoped, having only one arm as he did.

He stabbed out with his sword again. This time, he braced the pommel against his immobile right arm, giving it everything he had.

"GOROGOGOR?!?!"

Just for good measure. It didn't matter whether the creature could use spells or not. He wouldn't give it the chance.

He pushed his body weight even harder into the twitching form of the shaman and struck again, once more at the throat.

"—?! ——?!"

Again and again, until the shivering body stopped moving. Again. As many times as it took.

"..."

Then, finally, he let out a breath.

His sword was buried up to the hilt in the throat of the shaman, who had finally fallen still. His hand and fingers felt frozen solid; he simply stayed there with the sword tight in his grip.

"...Hrm."

With effort, he managed to free his fingers from the sword, coating the pommel with gore to lubricate it.

He looked around and saw, in the dim darkness, goblin corpses scattered all over. He was the only thing moving.

The goblin shaman, the hobgoblin, the rest of the goblins: they were all dead.

No.

He had killed them.

If he killed them, he would not be killed himself.

"……"

Silently, he grabbed the sword that was lodged in the corpse's throat; he braced his foot against the body to pull it out. But it was slick with blood, and he found he simply couldn't handle it with only one hand.

He grunted, looking around at the aftermath of the fight, then pulled out the dagger he had brought along as backup.

It was the only weapon he had left.

He forced his head, which wanted to lean to one side because of the missing horn, to stay straight, then somehow managed to prepare a torch with just his one hand.

By the light of its flame, he went back into the cave.

The place was full of bodies. Steam rose from innards, dark blood coated everything, and the empty eyes of dead goblins stared at him.

They were lucky there were even any bodies left, he thought. It was better than goblins deserved.

"Four by the entrance, and only…" he concluded, "…one chieftain. Five total."

He kicked one of the corpses, which rolled over on its back, clearly dead.

Or at least, it appeared to be dead.

So he raised his little dagger.

"Six."

One at a time, he drove the knife into their throats, carved them open, made sure they would never breathe again. If they were already dead, well and good. If they were mortally wounded, he finished them off. If they tried to ambush him, he killed them.

Doing all this with just his left arm was exhausting work. The dagger became so covered in blood that he thought it might slip from his hand, so he switched to a reverse grip and wrapped it around his hand with a bandage. He couldn't tie it, but as long as he had the least grip on the weapon, he wouldn't drop it.

Partway through his work, a stomach-churning stench and shocking pain in his right arm suddenly assailed him, making him feel faint. Was it seconds or minutes that he lay there? Or hours or days? In an instant, his consciousness snapped back into focus, and he vomited.

What had he fallen into? Waste, or blood, or both? He slowly rose to his feet.

With his one good arm, he searched through his bag, retrieving some potion-soaked herbs and pushing them into his mouth. They tasted disgusting, but as he chewed on them, he felt his mind growing slightly clearer. A few herbs wouldn't heal his wounds, though. He needed medical attention.

His right arm throbbed viciously, but pain was a sign that he had sensation. He could worry about it later.

After he had done everything he had to do.

"...Ten, eleven——— Twelve, thirteen, fourteen... Fifteen... Sixteen..."

It took an agonizingly long time, but he made sure that each goblin was dead. Pierce the throat, sunder it, then draw the dagger back and on to the next one. Time and again, he repeated the process.

He had no idea how long it was before he finally arrived at the deepest part of the cave.

He didn't immediately understand what he was looking at. The ceiling was high above him, the wind blowing through. Was the chamber natural, or had it been dug out? He had no idea. But the deserted room was obviously intended for some important person (or goblin). In the middle of the chamber, bound by chains, was a woman.

She was covered in filth and not moving a muscle.

If he remembered correctly—and if he hadn't been unconscious for very long—she had been abducted about a week earlier.

"...Are you alive?"

He saw a movement, so slight that at first he thought it was a trick of the flickering torchlight. But then he saw her breasts—covered in painful-looking bite marks—swell gently up and down, proof that the village girl was still living.

So now she was rescued, but her life had been wrecked.

"..."

Without a word, he knelt down beside her and checked her over, then silently stood up.

That wasn't for him to decide. He could only have faith.

Might she not have been happier to be killed by the goblins than to be rescued in this state? Killed by goblins—how could that be happiness? It was a foolish thought.

He looked around the chamber, noting several spots that seemed like places where a goblin might still be hiding. The corner, for example. An altar stood there as if designed to draw attention, although it appeared to be a pale imitation of some original. It was made of human bones. He kicked it down, the bones clattering to the ground, and then he looked all around it.

"..."

He found his goblins.

Several small creatures, huddled together, shaking and jabbering in thin voices. Were they begging for their lives?

He gazed at the monsters, cowering in the corner of the room.

Tiny goblins. Children. Goblin children.

He was sure the adults had told them to hide. He could imagine it easily.

He recognized their expressions: they looked at him the way anyone would look at someone who burst into their home.

He cocked his head as if thinking about something and stood for a long moment.

The goblin children started to pick up rocks in their miniature hands. Did they think he couldn't see them?

He took a breath in, and then let it out. He detected the already familiar scent, a mixture of rotten flesh and waste and mud.

He looked around, listening to the shallow breathing of the village girl, utterly robbed of her dignity.

With a slow nod, he counted the goblins up.

"Twenty-one."

Then he brought his dagger down.

§

She looked at the twilight sun that to her seemed the color of blood.

It sank in the west, turning the sky red.

Every time she saw it as she followed the cows around the farm, she averted her gaze.

Have I always done that?

Yes, probably. She hated twilight. She loved the night sky but couldn't stand the sight of the setting sun.

I wonder why that is.

The reason was different now than it had been before. Even she understood that much.

When she was little, it had been because she didn't want to go home. Playtime was over when the sun set. She had to part ways with *him* and go home. For some reason, it upset her every time.

But now…

"I guess this isn't the time to be thinking about it."

She had to hurry and get the cows back to the barn. Cow Girl shook her head. Her long hair billowed. She had decided to grow it long for herself, but there were times when it could be quite annoying.

"Oh, come on," she grumbled, sweeping her hair out of the way. She went after the cows, calling, "*Come on, cows!*"

She looked up to see the long shadows of people passing by the farm along the road. Their shadows reached out eerily, legs and arms stretching unnaturally.

Merchants, travelers, adventurers. Yes—adventurers. And among them, an exceptionally strange-looking one.

He was covered by armor and a helmet, carrying a shield and sword, clear markers of an adventurer.

That was well and good, but his entire body was covered in grime. One of the horns had broken off his helmet, his shield was in tatters, and his sword didn't seem to be quite right. On top of all that, he stank. Some people grimaced as he passed; others laughed at him behind their hands.

He didn't seem like trouble. Just another novice who had bitten off more than he could chew and wound up dragging himself back home. Nobody could grow without struggle, just like how a child could never learn to stand without falling down.

The reaction, though, was only human: when people saw someone in dire straits, they either pitied them or mocked them.

Cow Girl was the former, feeling sorry for the adventurer. She frowned.

I wonder if he's hurt.

One of his arms hung limply, and he was dragging one foot as he walked silently along. It was painful just to look at him.

But that was all there was to it; it wasn't like she felt anything special for him.

Anyway, it was just some injured adventurer walking along the road. Was there anything special about it?

Then he passed by the farm, heading for town, and with a little distance between them, she saw his back and stopped.

"Wha...?"

The stick she used to guide the animals fell from Cow Girl's hand. She couldn't explain it—she just had a feeling. A foolish feeling. But on reflection, maybe no other explanation was necessary.

If. Just *if.*

If he had survived, I'm sure he would have—

—become an adventurer...!

No sooner had the thought crossed her mind than Cow Girl was running. She jumped the fence, completely forgetting about the cows.

It was only a short distance to the road, but she refused to blink, feeling as though he might disappear if she did.

"H-hey, hey, you! Wait—Just wait a second!"

He didn't stop or turn around. Maybe he didn't realize she was talking to him.

Cow Girl gritted her teeth and ran faster. She was sure she hadn't run so hard since she'd been a girl. She could never have gotten so far from the village, no matter how hard she'd run.

"I said, wait...!"

Almost before she realized it, she'd reached out her hand and grabbed his arm. She had been able to touch him.

She tugged on that arm, and finally, he stopped walking. She put her free hand on her chest and breathed a sigh. The way passersby were looking at them made her uncomfortable—but no matter.

The helmet turned toward her, and a red eye stared at her from behind the visor.

"Er, um..."

She couldn't see his expression at all, yet the eye seemed to pierce through her, and she swallowed hard.

"Hey, you... You remember me, don't you?"

Her voice shook. Would he recognize her? Or did she have the wrong person? Her hand trembled on his arm.

What would she do if she had made a mistake? It was a little too late for such doubts.

How ridiculous she would feel. How stupid. She bit her lip hard.

He inclined his helmet ever so slightly and, after a moment, in a terribly quiet and cold voice, murmured, "...Yes."

So it is *him!*

Cow Girl couldn't identify the emotion that flared up in her heart. She didn't know whether she was joyful or sad, but tears streamed down her face.

"Where's your house? Where are you staying? What have you been...? Are you all right? What about your sister?!"

She couldn't stop anymore. The words poured out of her; she shocked even herself with how much she spoke.

Five years. It had been five years. What could they talk about? What should she ask? What should she say or tell him?

At last, the seemingly endless stream of words stopped, stymied by his complete silence, the lack of even a whisper.

"Oh, um..." Now she was staring at his helmet, embarrassed.

And then he spoke. Easily, as though it were nothing unusual.

"...I was slaying goblins."

"Oh..."

She could hardly breathe.

Through her mind flashed the image of her parents' empty coffins, no bodies to bury at their funeral.

She remembered asking her uncle something. Him not telling her anything.

The wind grew stronger, sending a sigh through the grass of the farm.

This wind seemed so cold, so cruel.

"Um, I just..."

She removed her trembling hand from his arm. She was sure now that he wouldn't move even if she let go of him.

Cow Girl took in one deep breath, her chest expanding, then let it out. She didn't know what was best, but she knew what she could do. At least, she thought she did.

"W-wait right here, okay?"

"..."

He gave no answer. She thought, though, that meant "okay." It had to, she told herself.

She started off running, but after a few steps, she spun around.

"If you disappear, I'll never forgive you!"

Now she knew he was still there behind her. Rubbing her eyes, she kept on running.

He was just...standing there. Just as if he was waiting for his sister to come get him.

§

"Uncle!"

The owner of the farm looked up slowly as his niece threw the door of the house open with a bang. He had finished his day's work and had just been packing some tobacco shavings into his pipe to enjoy a moment's relaxation.

It was unusual for her to seem so out of sorts. In fact, he couldn't remember it happening before.

"The boy— The boy, he—!"

"There, now, calm down. Are you all right? Did something happen to you?" Her agitation caused him to half rise to his feet before he knew what he was doing.

This was his younger sister's daughter. She had known terrible misfortune. The owner of the farm was under no illusions that he could replace her parents, but he liked to think he had raised her with care.

There were a lot of rough people in town. Some of them were even adventurers: often, the lower ranks weren't so far removed from average street toughs. He felt a clinging fear that one of them had done something to his niece.

"N-no, no, it's n-not—"

But she shook her head vigorously, her hair flying every which way. The words spilled out in a trembling tone, almost as if she were crying.

"That boy... The boy from next door, he's alive... He's been alive all this time!"

"What?!" Her uncle jumped completely out of his chair. "Next door? You mean...from the village?!"

"Yes...!" Her face was a mess of tears that poured out of the corners of her eyes, but she nodded again and again. She managed to keep talking through her sniffles. "I g-guess he's an—an adven...venturer now... And he's right...out...!"

"An adventurer..." A cloud passed over the farm owner's face, and he shook his head. "Is he coming back from work?"

"I think... I think probably, yes..."

There were many rumors about adventurers, and not all could be believed. But novices to the trade were said to take one of two types of jobs: mucking out the sewers or...

"So he was slaying goblins, was he?"

"Yes..."

The owner saw his niece nod weakly. "Goblins. Of course." He let out a sort of deep groan.

Adventuring. Maybe the boy had had no other choice. The world was too cruel for an orphan to survive any other way. But still...an adventurer. And one involved with goblins, no less.

"I want to...let him stay...here, but..."

Maybe you won't let him. At the girl's question, the farm owner's face took on a pained expression, and he let out a sigh.

When I think of what that boy must have gone through, I guess it's only natural he'd want revenge.

The farm owner himself had lost family, after all. It wasn't as if he didn't understand the feeling.

As he recalled, his niece and the boy in question were close in age: he must be thirteen, or fourteen, or maybe fifteen...

Too young, in any event, to cope with such burgeoning emotions.

Suppose someone passing by in the street punched you in the face, then simply walked away smiling. Few people would forgive such an act, let alone forget it. But to then hunt down the person who had hit you, and hit them back—how much time and effort would that take? And how much the more so if there was an 80 or 90 percent chance that someone had already dealt with that person?

I suppose he'll feel better after he's destroyed two or three nests.

That would be the limit of it, the farm owner decided. That would be all. Otherwise, where would it end?

If he decides he wants to learn a respectable trade, he can help me on the farm.

And above all, it was his niece's request.

Ever since he had taken her in, she had been given to keeping her eyes down, never letting her feelings be known. Now she had come to him with a desperate wish. How could he trample on her emotions?

"...Fine." The farm owner let out a long, deep breath, the crags of his sunbaked face breaking into a smile. "Tell him he may stay. For tonight. For as many nights as he pleases."

"You really mean it?!"

How did that proverb go? "The crow who was just crying now cackles with laughter."

The girl's face was shining, even as her tears still glistened in her eyes.

"*However,*" her uncle said, "I will need him to pay rent. That will make sure he's at least somewhat invested in this place."

The farm owner didn't forget this word of admonishment. His niece obviously trusted the boy, but as her guardian, he had to be more careful. It had been five years since her home had been destroyed, more than enough time for the boy to become not just an adventurer but a ruffian, one of those unsavory creatures.

He could stay in a barn or someplace until the owner was more certain of who he was now.

"If he can accept that, then bring him here."

"R-right! That's perfect!"

His niece rubbed her eyes repeatedly with her sleeve. They were red and swollen, and she blinked to clear them.

"I'll—I'll be right back with him! Thank you, Uncle!"

Then she spun and flew out the door even faster than she had come in.

The door closed with a slam. The farm owner looked at it and sighed yet again.

"Now, then..."

She had been in such a rush; he was sure she had forgotten to bring the cows home.

He would have to do it for her. The farm owner gave a great stretch and got ready for work.

This boy wasn't a total stranger. He wasn't blood, just his niece's friend, but a bond was a bond. He came from the same village.

Who knows? If we show him a nice, quiet life, maybe it'll temper his feelings as well.

Then the farm owner went outside, having no idea how wrong he was.

§

The stars gleamed in the night sky, and the twin moons shone brightly.

He was looking up, staring intently at the red and green moons.

In the distance could be heard the last of the day's hubbub from town, a din that stretched from the dark depths of the forest to the grass of the farm's fields. If one listened closely, one might even hear the voices of wild beasts hiding among the shadows.

But listening closely was not what he was doing.

He was simply standing, replaying the battle in his mind.

He had prepared his equipment, gone into the cave, fought the goblins, and killed them.

He could still feel in his hands the sensation of having taken twenty-one lives. He wasn't used to it yet.

He had carried the girl out and delivered her to the village chief. He didn't know what happened to her after that, nor did he care to ask.

He didn't think of it in terms of having won or lost. He didn't even think of it as having rescued someone.

All he knew was that he had destroyed a nest.

What did he think would come of obliterating a single goblin hole?

Nothing.

All he had done was destroy one goblin nest.

Nothing more.

Nothing had changed.

Of course it hadn't. Had he expected it would, even a little? Ridiculous.

His heart felt cold. Not so much as a ripple of emotion ran through it.

I have much to think about.

His sword had broken, but it turned out to be more convenient that way. He would need to procure a short sword.

His armor satisfied him, but it seemed to be vulnerable to stabs. He would need a fine chain mail or the like.

A shield had been the right choice. Ideally, it would be a little smaller and easier to move… One with no handle, just a strap.

The helmet was important. It had saved his life. But what to do about the horns…or horn?

Antidotes. Potions. Healing items. He would require a variety of such things. It was many against one. He needed every ace he could get.

He would have to think of a strategy. If he kept doing what he had done this time, he would die. He didn't mind dying, but he wanted to take more than one or two of *them* with him.

Tactics were important, too. He would have to be able to kill more goblins more precisely, and without leaving the job half-done.

If he could kill them, he wouldn't be killed. The truth was as simple as that.

He would think, plan, and attack. He could not ignore continued training.

There were no guarantees that things would immediately go well. But he would do better next time. And better still the time after that.

It would not end with one or two nests. It couldn't.

This was the beginning. Only his first step.

I'm going to kill all the goblins.

"Heeeey!"

That was when she arrived: a girl rushing down the dark path without so much as a lantern, her chest heaving from exertion.

It was the girl who had stopped him. He remembered her. She had said, "Wait right here," and so he had waited.

"M-my un...uncle, he—he says—!"

He was sure he imagined the look of relief and joy that seemed to pass over her face when she saw him.

"He says you can...stay here! S-so let's—

"Let's go." The words were so soft, so strained, that it seemed she was about to burst into tears.

He was silent a moment, thinking. And then, he slowly nodded.

INTERLUDE

Of the Two of Them After That

"Whaaat?! And you let him go alone?!"

"I guess that was a mistake, huh…"

"Not exactly a mistake, but… There's no way to know if he'll be all right."

"I swear, I didn't know he was really going to solo it."

"Well, just be careful next time."

"Right… Next time…"

"That's all we have, isn't it? If you're going to get this upset about it, just make extra sure!"

"Right…"

"Look, here comes a new adventurer. He looks…odd. Or…weird."

"He does… Wha?!"

"…"

"Uh, um… Can I…? Can I help you?"

"Goblins."

"Sorry?"

"There were goblins."

CHAPTER 4

Middle Phase

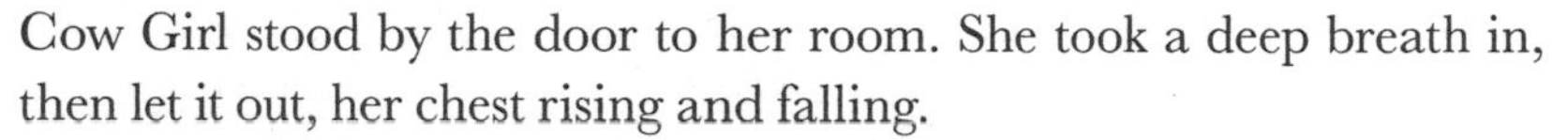

Cow Girl stood by the door to her room. She took a deep breath in, then let it out, her chest rising and falling.

The sun sent its rays streaming through the window, and she could hear a rooster crowing mightily. She was up earlier than usual today, dressed and ready to go. Everything was set. All she needed now was her resolve.

"O-okay...!"

She clenched her fist in a show of determination, then turned the doorknob and opened the door.

"G-good morning! The sun's up! ...Erk."

She burst into the room as brightly as she could—only to find it empty.

A "neat room" sounds like a nice idea, but it's easy to be neat when the only things in a room are a bed made from a pile of straw, and a chair.

The blanket was folded neatly on the straw pile; it showed no sign of having been used.

Cow Girl scratched her cheek in embarrassment. It seemed she had completely missed him.

"I guess he went out already..."

Or had he not yet come back?

She settled her shapely bottom on the straw pile and heaved a sigh.

He left at random times and came back at random times. She hardly ever saw him.

"...There are so many things I'd like to talk to him about, though."

The way things were, it was as if they really were just renting him a room.

"Are adventurers that busy?"

She didn't know.

She lived right down the street from a town that hosted a branch of the Adventurers Guild, yet she didn't know anything about them at all.

There were too many things she didn't know. Why was that? Here she had been, living in this town for five years.

It's because I never go out.

Cow Girl bit her lip and stood up. She quickly smoothed out the sheets where she had disturbed them, then she flung the door open and barged into the kitchen. Determination starts from the feet up.

Her uncle was just putting some tobacco into his pipe, relaxing for a moment after breakfast. "Well, you're up early," he said, looking at her.

"Uncle, do you have any deliveries to make in town today?" She blurted the words out, feeling like if she talked about anything else at all first, she might lose her nerve.

"Hmm. Well, yes, I do..." He seemed slightly taken aback by his niece's forcefulness. His chair rattled as he nodded. "Why do you ask?"

"I'm going with you!"

You had to start with the first step. Her uncle stared wide-eyed as Cow Girl clenched her fist in determination.

§

"Uggggh..."

The new Guild girl gave an exhausted sigh and pressed her forehead into the counter. Around her was a mountain of paperwork. They were all requests for adventurers brought in that day. Some, Guild Girl had written down herself, while others were from other employees.

She grabbed a random page near her head and saw the inevitable words: *goblin slaying.*

It was enough to make anyone sigh.

"Hey, now, don't slack off!" her coworker said, giving her a rap on the head.

"But..."

Her coworker was also a cleric, and she always seemed alert. Guild Girl couldn't help feeling jealous. She assumed her coworker would at some point officially be given the position of inspector, as well.

As for herself, Guild Girl didn't feel it would be possible for her to petition the gods earnestly enough to evoke a miracle.

"There are so many goblin quests here, we're never going to get through them all."

"'So many'? I'd say there's about as many as usual."

"Well, that's true, but..." Guild Girl pursed her lips and straightened the stack of papers.

The proverb held that every time a party of new adventurers was formed, a goblin nest appeared. Goblin-slaying quests were so common and so endless that they could even give rise to popular wisdom like that.

There were plenty of quests that dealt with bandits, or trolls, or lamias, or harpies. But broken down by monster type, goblin quests seemed to Guild Girl to be by far the most prevalent.

"Just let the newbies handle them," her coworker said.

"I could, but..." Guild Girl listlessly picked up a pen. "There aren't any promises it would work out for them."

"They have to take responsibility for themselves."

This time, she gave Guild Girl a gentle smack on the cheek, eliciting a little *yeep!*

"Okay, so I won't go that far. But risk is part of adventuring, isn't it?"

"True..."

"We just take the quests, assign them to adventurers, and if they succeed, we give them their rewards and our trust. Right?"

"I guess so."

Well, as long as you understand. Her coworker promptly turned back to her own counter.

The Guild was already bustling with adventurers who had come seeking work. There wasn't time to sit and chat.

Guild Girl flipped through the pages she had yet to post on the bulletin board and sighed once more.

This reward is barely enough... Not that a village like that can afford to offer much more...

There were requests from destitute places, farming villages, pioneer towns. They were offering every coin they could scrape together, and it was still pocket change to experienced adventurers.

As a result, the work often fell to newly minted monster hunters, those with the lowest rank, Porcelain, or the ninth rank, Obsidian. They might fail, but the goblins would still be eliminated. The second, or perhaps the third, party would destroy the nest.

Part of what made an adventurer good at their job was the ability to pick quests that matched their strength, gear, and party composition. They were ultimately responsible for their own success or failure. The Guild didn't have the resources to coddle every last dreamer who showed up to register.

It's a way of weeding them out, I guess...

But if that was true, then it became a question of whether they could let the lawless and the violent continue to flourish.

Whoever she picked, though, she was still sending someone off to face their doom.

Maybe I'm in the wrong line of work.

Still unable to get her emotions under control, Guild Girl tried to force a smile onto her face. Just in front of her was a massive adventurer, presumably come to find work for the day. He shoved his face close to hers.

"Yo there. Got any troll-slaying quests? Now, there's a way to earn a quick buck."

"I'm very sorry, there aren't any trolls today..." Guild Girl frowned, and she flipped through her papers. A dim hope flashed through her mind. "Perhaps a goblin quest...?"

"Goblins?" The hulking adventurer was unimpressed. "Goblins don't pay, and they're no fun. Let the Porcelains handle 'em."

Just for a second, Guild Girl bit her lip. It was about the reaction she'd expected. She couldn't—and shouldn't—force the matter.

"I'm sorry, sir..."

She was just bowing her head apologetically when a voice broke in.

"Goblins?"

Guild Girl had no idea how long he'd been there. The adventurer shuffled out from behind the huge man, his voice low and mechanical. He wore grimy leather armor and a steel helmet with one horn broken off, along with a small, round shield on his arm and a sword of a strange length at his hip. The equipment all looked thoroughly used, suggesting he had been through several adventures already.

Guild Girl had dealt with him several times and already recognized him. How could she not? The shock she'd received when he came back from soloing that goblin nest seared him into her memory.

But she had never known him to jump into a conversation like this. She blinked several times.

The question came again: "Goblins?"

"Er, yes." It was all Guild Girl could do to nod her head.

"I see," he whispered dispassionately. "If there are goblins involved, I'll go."

"Oh-ho, lookit little Porcelain boy here," the big adventurer said, glancing dubiously at the armored boy. "Didn't you take on a goblin-killing quest the other day?"

"Yes." He nodded. "I did."

The huge adventurer just let out a breath and nodded disinterestedly, but then a smile came over his face. "Well, that works for me. I'll take this one, then." He glanced at the papers on Guild Girl's counter and grabbed one. "Get rid of the wizard on Firetop Mountain? Sounds good."

"Er, yes, sir! I understand he's in an underground maze, so please be careful." Guild Girl took care of the quest acceptance with a certain measure of urgency. She had to explain the reward, outline the quest content, and then make sure the adventurer really wanted and accepted the quest. Then her part was over.

Recently, she had finally started to feel accustomed to the routine, and this time she was somehow able to fill out the paperwork without a hitch. *Phew.* A sigh of relief.

"Goblins or giant rats are a good way to cut your teeth," the big adventurer said as he left. "Good luck, kid."

The adventurer in the helmet watched him go without much interest, then turned back to the counter.

"So, the goblins?"

Yikes...

For a moment, she found herself set back on her heels: deep within that expressionless steel mask, she could see a glowing red eye.

Guild Girl shook her head to clear it. She had to get the smile back on her face.

"Are there no goblins?"

"N-no, there are..." She couldn't help smiling a little, for real, at his reaction. She cleared her throat, forcing herself to focus. "We have goblin-slaying quests. Several of them, in fact."

"I see. So there *are* goblins."

What's with this guy?

She didn't know the answer, but even as she looked at him in perplexity, she pulled several papers from the pile of quests.

She had encountered a wide range of adventurers, both during her training at the capital and since being assigned to this town. Some were strange, some had their particular obsessions, some were full of themselves. A whole panoply of personalities.

But he's...different somehow.

"E-er, so here's one to start with. Goblins took some village livestock and injured the young man on guard..."

"I accept."

He nodded, his response instantaneous. He didn't ask about the reward but made to take the paper from Guild Girl's hand, almost as if he were going to steal it.

"Two or three of them?"

"Um... May I explain about the reward?"

"Yes." He didn't sound all that interested.

"Hmm," Guild Girl said, frowning just a little. "I need you to listen to me, or I could get in trouble myself."

"Is that so?"

"Yes, it is." She nodded, putting on a serious face. She was dealing with someone who was used to a little fighting. If there was a dispute about the reward, it was the Guild girls who were standing in the line of fire. Even back in the capital, they had emphasized how important it was not to appear intimidated.

"Trust and goodwill," she said. "This is a job, and we are paying you, so please complete it to the best of your ability." She raised her pointer finger as if offering a lesson, but the truth was, Guild Girl herself didn't completely understand what she was saying. "And think about this: without a reward, you couldn't pay your rent or buy food or equipment, could you?"

Hence, she added a comment about the reward to the best of her understanding. It wasn't anything revelatory; it was the sort of thing anyone would have known. But *he* lapsed into thought, until finally, a soft grunt came from inside the helmet.

"...In that case, I will listen." He nodded. Guild Girl put a hand to her chest in relief.

Thank goodness he went along with me.

This wasn't the first time she had worked with him. Each time, he chose goblin slaying.

Maybe it was because he was a beginner. She was still surprised that he hadn't formed a party, but regardless, he was a big help to her. Even then, though, she knew that someday his rank would increase, and he would go on to fight bigger, more powerful monsters.

That's just how things are around here.

"Thank you for your continued patronage!"

He was going to walk out that door and, quite possibly, into the jaws of death. This might be her only chance to express her gratitude.

She bowed, her braids bouncing, but he only cocked his head. It was almost as if he couldn't fathom why she was thanking him.

He seems surprisingly...decent.

The passing thought was a little flippant, and she let it go as she launched into her explanation to this increasingly familiar adventurer.

§

"Hey, he went that way!"

"Yikes, h-he's gonna get away!"

"Surround 'em, that'll make it easy!"

"But don't let down your guard. Goblins are monsters, too!"

The party of four adventurers was putting their weapons to work on the twilit outskirts of the village.

"Don't think I don't know it!"

Their leader had only just registered as an adventurer the other day. He swung his two-handed sword mightily, jumping into the fray.

"GROORB?! GOORBGBORG?!"

A goblin with an armful of vegetables gibbered and ran, screaming as the sword took him. The vegetables dropped on the ground, splitting open, but then, so did the goblin. His innards splattered among the produce. The adventurers' leader looked away with distaste.

"Guess nobody'll be having those for dinner..."

"Look out! Over there!" *There's another one!* It was the voice of their ranger girl. Her ears were somewhat pointy: she was a half-elf.

She was pointing to where a goblin was charging into the forest, carrying a lamb.

"Gnomes! Undines! Make for me the finest cushion you will see!"

The half-elf had some communion with the spirits of the four directions, even if not as much as a full elf. She grabbed the canteen at her hip and poured water out of it; it danced and splashed on the ground.

Guided by her almost singsongy words, the water merged with the spirits of the earth, forming mud and catching the goblin's feet.

"GROORB?!"

The Snare spell stopped the creature cold. The lamb struggled out of his arms and ran away.

"Hah, you're mine now...!" Another warrior approached, lifting an ax. His body, rippling with muscles, looked like the side of a cliff. He was a dwarf.

The blade of his ax smashed into the goblin's skull, sending brains everywhere. The monster gave one great spasm and died. A splash of the creature's blood got in the dwarf's beard, but he only laughed aloud as he braced himself against the corpse and pulled out his weapon.

"We're even on kills now!"

"Just you wait. I'll win next time," the leader shot back. He shook his sword to get the blood off, then put it back in its scabbard. He kept the blade at his hip, because he had found that with the sword across his back, he couldn't get to it quickly enough when he needed it.

"You will be relieved to know that no one appears to be injured," said their monk. The bald-pated follower of the God of Knowledge placed a grateful hand to his chest.

The party had been on several adventures, but they had all involved investigating ruins. This had been their first field battle. Driving off a handful of goblins wasn't that big a deal, but they were still glad not to suffer any wounded.

"What about you, sir?" the monk asked.

"No problems," *he* responded dispassionately.

"He" was an undeniably pitiful-looking adventurer. He wore a steel helmet with one horn missing, grimy leather armor, and a small, round shield strapped to his arm. In his hand was a sword of a strange length, the blade currently buried in a goblin's brain.

"One," he said, giving the blade a ruthless twist and severing the spinal column with a sickening crack.

"You took two. Three all together."

"Right. The vegetables are a loss, but at least we got the lamb back. That's well and good."

"Ain't it?" the leader asked with a smile, eliciting agreement and a grin from the half-elf girl holding the small animal. The lamb squirmed as if it might get away from where she held it against her small chest, but despite her thin arms, she gave the animal no chance of escape.

"Geez. What I wouldn't give to be where he is. Why d'you suppose he's so upset?"

"What you wouldn't give?" the girl said, confused at first, but then she figured it out and exclaimed, "Why, you!" and puffed out her cheeks.

"Sorry, sorry," their warrior-leader said. The half-elf's expression softened immediately, and she stroked the lamb's head.

The dwarf shook his head at the sweet little scene. "Well, that's goblins for you." Ax resting across his shoulders, he gave a disinterested snort.

"I see," *he* said. He put his boot on the goblin's corpse and pulled out his sword, then used the tip to roll the body over. The creature was brutally thin, its rib cage prominently visible. A disgusting stench rose up from its filthy form.

"It doesn't appear to come from a nest," he said.

The monk ran a hand across his bald head as he looked at the body. Then he began to poke at the corpse gently with a finger. (Perhaps he was more used to such things than the others?)

"I agree," he said. "This creature is severely malnourished. Terribly thin. Perhaps a vagabond, or a Wanderer?"

"A 'Wanderer'?" *He* shook the blood off his sword and sheathed it, turning his one-horned helmet toward the monk.

"Like a bear with no den, the word describes a goblin with no nest."

"Is there anything else?"

"Er..." The monk touched his head again, then shook it. He had a strained smile on his face. "I'm afraid I don't know that much about goblins."

"I see." That was all he said before the helmet returned to gazing at the goblin body.

The leader watched him with interest, then slapped a friendly hand on his shoulder. "You're doing goblin slaying to get money for equipment, aren't you?"

The next quest's going to be a little tougher was his advice.

"Is that so?" was all *he* said. "Is it goblins?"

"Hell no," the leader said, looking confused. "The quest is to explore a mine."

"Yeah, I heard they stopped getting gold out of it," Half-Elf Girl said.

"The suspicion is that there's a monster down there," Dwarf Warrior added.

Elves and dwarves had been known to have a contentious relationship ever since mythical times, but maybe the same didn't hold true with half-elves and dwarves.

The dwarf squinted beneath his big, bushy eyebrows and eyed their companion. "Gotta say, I never expected to run into another adventurer."

It was fair enough: the goblins that were now rotting in the sun had probably been attacking any nearby villages without much thought. So one village requested their extermination, and a party accepted; another village requested defense, and a lone adventurer took them up on it.

It didn't really matter, so long as everyone could get their reward.

"This has to be more than just chance," the party leader said affably. "This guy and I registered on the exact same day, after all!" He gave the armored adventurer another hearty smack on the shoulder. "Hey, you're solo, right? How about you come with us on our next—"

"No," he said curtly. "Goblins."

Then he drew his dagger. As if it were no big deal, he sliced open the stomach of one of the monsters, like a hunter skinning his catch.

Half-Elf Girl choked a little, while the monk frowned and said, "Sir, what are you doing?"

"Investigating," he replied calmly, not interrupting his mechanical movements as he pulled out some organ or other. "I don't know much about goblins, either."

The party looked at one another as if they had discovered some unidentified being deep in a labyrinth. They could hardly be blamed for collectively deciding to move along.

He spent the entire night in that field, making sure no goblin reinforcements arrived, and then went home.

©Shingo Adachi

§

"Wh... Whoa..." Cow Girl nearly felt dizzy at all the activity.

They were at the Adventurers Guild—and there were so many adventurers there. It was after noon, and the crowd had thinned somewhat, but to Cow Girl, the confusion was still overwhelming.

People of every race, class, and age group, carrying every conceivable type of weapon, wandered around the lobby. She had seen dwarves and rheas in passing on the street, but elves she had heard of only in stories. Cow Girl was left blinking by the beauty of a passing elf girl.

She knew it was rude to stare, but she did anyway, maybe because she felt she would never have a chance to get any closer to an elf than this.

"All right then, I'm going to go make the deliveries. Just wait here quietly."

Her uncle's words brought her back to herself, and she quickly nodded and said, "Oh, uh, r-right!"

Her uncle headed for the reception desk, leaving Cow Girl standing there. That was when she noticed it.

They're looking at me.

Maybe she was somehow unusual, or just looked out of place, but passing adventurers kept stealing glances at her. She felt a flush run up her cheeks; she squeezed her eyes shut and kept her face down.

I knew I shouldn't have come here...

She fidgeted uncomfortably, finding herself unbearably embarrassed. When she finally peeked out from beneath her bangs, she spotted some benches, apparently a waiting area.

That would be a good place, Cow Girl thought. She would know right away when her uncle came back.

She worked her way over to the seats, trying to remain as inconspicuous as possible while also trying to appear as if she was used to this. Her nervousness made her hands and arms unwilling to move; she had no idea what to do with her sense of embarrassment. Somehow, though, she made it to the benches, sat down, and breathed a sigh of relief.

Thank goodness no one talked to me.

Placing a grateful hand to her burgeoning chest, Cow Girl finally got a proper look around the Guild. On a whim, she tried looking for *him* but saw no sign of that armor and helmet.

Still, though… Look at all the people here.

"Gawd, that was a real mess."

"It's all because you insisted on using that gigantic thing in such a small space. You should take a page from my book."

"Forget about Mister and Miss there. What's our next quest?"

"You could stand to learn a thing or two yourself. But anyway, um, I think it's investigating some mine. A big group effort."

"I hear slimes or something keep showing up there."

Cow Girl watched the party's animated discussion without really meaning to. The warrior carrying the giant sword—a broadsword, really—across his back seemed to be in charge.

Would *he* gather companions to himself like that one day? Or maybe he already had a party to go with him on his adventures.

And if he does…

Then, she had to admit, she would feel left out. Just a little.

"Is something the matter?"

"Eeyikes!"

The unexpected question made Cow Girl jump. She looked up, trying to calm her pounding heart, and saw a concerned-looking staff member.

The young woman appeared to be perhaps a little older than Cow Girl. Her braided hair made her look grown-up.

"I'm sorry," she said, "I certainly didn't mean to startle you…" Her shapely eyebrows furrowed.

"Oh, no, I'm sorry, too. I didn't mean to be so startled!" Cow Girl gave a wave of her hand. "Er, uh, my uncle—" Now she was embarrassed again. "Um, that is, you see…" She looked down, her face bright red.

She was completely tongue-tied. Was it the nervousness or the touch of panic?

She took a deep breath. The staff member waited politely for her. Then Cow Girl managed to say, "I'm from the farm…"

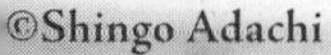
©Shingo Adachi

"Oh!" The staff member's face brightened. "Thank you for always bringing us produce!"

"Uh, and—and so…"

Why didn't I ever talk to more people?

It was too late for regrets. She would have to work with what she had.

If she couldn't speak now, she felt, she would never be able to speak. She would never be able to do anything.

Come on, tongue, work!

"I'm going to—to start coming to help my uncle, so, uh…!"

She forced her voice out as powerfully as she could but found herself short on words. She knew what she wanted to say but couldn't quite figure out how to say it.

Even as Cow Girl struggled to talk, the staff member smiled broadly. "Certainly. We look forward to working with you!"

The words were a godsend. "M-me too…!" Cow Girl blurted out, and Guild Girl, still smiling, gave her a perfect bow. Then she walked away, the gentle curve of her hips and bottom swaying as she moved, leaving Cow Girl to let out a breath.

She's such a lady…

Did men prefer girls like…like that?

After a very long moment, Cow Girl closed her fist gently and whispered, "I'll just have to do my best."

§

When *he* walked through the door of the Guild, silence descended immediately.

He entered the building at a bold stride, his boots covered in gruesome dark stains. The adventurers standing around could smell the reek rolling off him, and with every step he took, they turned to one another and whispered.

"Wow. So *that's* the guy…"

"They say he dissected a goblin. Maybe he wanted to sell its liver somewhere."

"Goblin slaying on his own? That's gutsy…"

"This is his second or third time, right? Isn't it about time he moved on from goblins?"

Apparently, the other adventurers, who had come back first, had been spreading gossip.

The outcome of an adventure was news that traveled quickly. But even so, he was very conspicuous. Part of an adventurer's job was to stand out.

"If he's got scout or ranger abilities, or maybe fighter levels, I could see inviting him with us."

"Ugh, pass. I don't want anyone chopping up any monsters in front of me."

"Is he even human? He looks too tall for a rhea…"

"Is he a *he*? Are you sure it's not a woman?"

"No, I'm sure he's a man… Wanna bet on it?"

"You're on."

Each adventurer looked at him with a different emotion: curiosity, suspicion, interest. But all of them whispered.

He, however, didn't even slow down but marched up to the reception desk.

"Now, I've just gotta make my report to my dear receptionist and— Yeek!" The spear-wielding adventurer found his mood suddenly spoiled. He gave the armored man a pointed glare but jumped out of the way.

The person in the armor didn't spare a glance at Spearman but continued ever forward. Had he interrupted something? No, he hadn't.

Spearman worked his mouth open and shut as if he wanted to say something, but Witch gently tugged on his arm to silence him.

I've got to admit, he does sort of look like an undead when you first see him.

Guild Girl had been watching everything.

She took a deep breath. She put a hand to her chest (of which she was secretly quite proud) and took another. She made sure she was smiling.

"Welcome back! How did the quest go?"

"Goblins appeared," he reported, then went quiet. Guild Girl's smile took on a frozen quality.

"Erm…" *Scritch, scratch.* She dipped the quill pen in a jar of ink and made a few notes on a piece of paper.

Wh-what do I do now?

She turned to the next counter looking for help, but her coworker appeared to be busy with another adventurer. In fact, *his* appearance had caused many of those waiting in line to drift elsewhere.

A-anyway. I just need to fill out the paperwork, that's all…

"How m-many goblins were there?"

"Three. They had no weapons."

"Right, then. Three, no equipment. Got it."

That was in accordance with the quest description, which claimed that three or so goblins had shown up.

Guild Girl focused on writing as neatly as she could, the pen scratching along the report paper.

"……"

The entire time, the steel helmet faced resolutely in her direction, with no sign of moving.

H-he's making it hard to work…!

She wasn't exactly embarrassed or shy, but she was having trouble enduring the situation.

Anyway, as quest completion reports went, "killed three goblins" left something to be desired.

Guild Girl strengthened her determination as if she were facing a dragon, then confronted the strange adventurer.

"How did y-you defeat them?"

"Another party had already taken up a quest. They eliminated two of the goblins, and I one," he replied with an uncommon lack of embellishment. Guild Girl blinked, thrown off her rhythm.

Okay, then… She asked the next question with hesitancy in her voice:

"Is there anything else…?"

"Else?"

"You know, uh, anything you noticed, or anything else you did?"

He paused for a moment, then said softly, "I watched for a full night. But I saw no evidence of reinforcements." The steel helmet tilted thoughtfully.

Guild Girl gave him a questioning look, whereupon he added,

again quietly, "The other party's monk suggested they might have been Wanderers. Goblins who have lost their nest."

"I see, I see…"

Huh. As Guild Girl kept her pen moving across the paper, her expression began to soften. The boy was reticent and a little odd.

What a strange guy. But hey, if you ask him a question, he's sure to answer.

He did the job he was asked to do. And he returned after completing it.

Guild Girl asked him one probing question after another, nodding and writing as he answered.

"Let me make sure I have this right, then. You accepted the quest and arrived at the location, whereupon you encountered three goblins."

"That's right." The steel helmet nodded. It made Guild Girl think of a bobblehead doll, and she smiled.

"You joined up with another party that was already there on another assignment. Together, you all slew three goblins. You detected no indication of reinforcements."

"Correct."

"In that case, the quest is complete. Good work!"

The smile Guild Girl gave him was not one of her pasted-on expressions. It came over her face very naturally.

Looking over her notes, Guild Girl opened the safe in the prescribed manner and took out the pouch of reward money: the reward for goblin slaying. Money the people of that village had scrimped and saved to offer.

It might weigh less when she converted the coins, but that didn't take away from the emotions the money embodied.

She placed it on a tray and set it on the counter. He stared at it for a moment, then nonchalantly picked up the money.

"Just like I told you, right? You take a job, you do the job, then you get a reward."

Hmph! She made a triumphant little sound and puffed out her chest (of which she was secretly quite proud), holding up her pointer finger as if offering a lesson.

"That's an adventurer's responsibility—his trust and goodwill."

Her coworker gave her a weary look as if to ask what she was blathering about, but Guild Girl paid her no mind. She was happy that the boy before her had slain the goblins, that she had paid the reward, and that their business was successfully concluded.

In her mind's eye, Guild Girl could still see the worried farmer standing at the reception desk. What a relief this would be for the villagers.

How wonderful that she had been a small part of it. That she had been able to send him out to—

"So. Do you have any goblin quests?"

"...Sorry—?"

Guild Girl had just been straightening some papers on the desk and thought she had misheard.

"Goblins." The steel helmet looked directly at her.

From the next desk over, Spearman was looking at them incredulously.

Is there something wrong with this guy?

She couldn't keep the thought from passing through her head, and no doubt she wasn't the only one. Adventurers all over the Guild had been keeping one ear on the conversation, and now they stared agape.

Guild Girl swallowed. She thought it sounded awfully loud. Her voice shook as she said, "G-goblins...?"

"Yes." There was no quaver as he answered. Did he see the ripple of uncertainty in her own expression? The helmet tilted slightly and he said, "I will accept a reward."

Was that his way of saying he understood how things worked now? Or was he trying to imply that what he decided to do was his business?

There were the novices who went out to slay goblins, and all the people who came by each day to request adventurers to slay those goblins.

There were the ones who never came back, and all those who refused the quests.

And then there was the one person who both accepted the quests and came back.

Guild Girl bit her lip for a long moment, but then let out a breath.

This was simply the way things had turned out.

If they were going to ask him for help, they would have to help him in return. Guild Girl dipped her pen in her inkwell again.

The Guild was no charity, but there was no reason not to help an adventurer.

At least, there shouldn't be, right?

"Goblins?"

"Yes, we have several goblin quests."

Although he may not have noticed how she was feeling, she didn't have to force herself to smile at him.

So it goes. A natural smile would have to do. No, that's not enough.

"Could I ask you to be a bit more proactive in your report next time?"

"Erm..."

She found herself at the mercy of a steel helmet whose thoughts she couldn't read. In that case, she had a thing or two to say to him.

"Is it true you dissected a goblin?"

"I did..."

"Well, perhaps you could avoid actions that are likely to be misunderstood by civilians and other adventurers." Her smile didn't falter as she spoke.

"Erm," he grunted.

Is he actually at a loss?

Guild Girl wanted to have just a little more fun. And honestly, she was curious.

"Why in the world would you do something like that, anyway?"

"To learn."

"Learn what?"

"About goblins."

Guild Girl couldn't understand why a person would be so fixated on goblins.

Goblins, goblins, goblins. Guild Girl rolled the barrel of her pen against her temples.

"Please don't do that in the future. At least, not when it could cause misunderstandings."

She added "As I'm sure you're already aware" with a smile tugging at the edges of her lips.

§

Cow Girl awoke to a sound sometime before dawn, while the sky was still a dark blue.

"Hr…nn…"

She squirmed in her bed, until just her head was poking out from under her blanket, and looked out the window.

Sunrise was still some way off; it was that numinous moment between full dark and dawn. Even the roosters were still sleeping.

Yet, she was sure she had heard something. Footsteps. Faint but… bold, nonchalant.

"Is he…home?"

Being careful not to make any noise that might wake her uncle, Cow Girl slid out of bed.

Traces of nighttime still hung in the air, clinging to her bare skin without mercy, making her shiver.

She pulled on an ill-fitting undershirt and lit the wick of a candle. She crept quietly into the hallway and began walking hesitantly through the silent house.

She was already well on her way when she was seized by the fear that she might be wrong about the noise; she picked up a piece of firewood and held it in one hand.

"Um, uh…"

Finally, she arrived at his room. The door was shut tight; she swallowed heavily. She knocked gently, reluctantly, on the door, then she opened it a crack and peeked in.

"Welcome…home…?"

There was no answer. In fact, there was no sense that anyone was inside.

The bed still showed no sign of having been used. The blanket was folded neatly. There were hardly any belongings within.

Cow Girl took a careful step into the room, stirring up a thin layer of dust on the floor.

"…He's not here?"

But then the faint sound came again. It could have been nothing more than her imagination, a phantom of hope, but she was sure she heard it.

Inside the house—no.

"Outside… Maybe."

Come to think of it, didn't he say he would borrow the shed…?

The shed was ancient and had long gone unused. Could that be where the sound was coming from?

Cow Girl raised the collar of the shirt that was all she had on over her bare skin, then stepped out the front door and into the night.

Immediately, she was caught by a whistling dawn wind that felt like a knife on her skin. It was supposed to be spring now, but the gust felt like a last gasp of winter.

The candle guttered; Cow Girl hurriedly sheltered it with her hand and blew on it.

Maybe it's not quite proper, being outside dressed like this…

She dismissed the thought; it wasn't as if there was anyone there to see her.

The shed rose as a shadow against an ultramarine sky. The roof and walls were full of holes, and with the wind whipping through the grass all around, it looked deserted.

I guess I've never actually been in there…

She had the sense that the shed had always been like this, ever since she had come to the farm five years earlier. Had she gone into the shed when she was exploring on her first day here?

"Oof…"

Maybe she really had imagined the sound? Cow Girl took a step back.

There was no one there. There couldn't be. She had been crazy to come out here alone. The shed looked like a place that would attract goblins.

Goblins: "the little devils."

She had never seen the monsters, but the thought of them caused her to shake her head, her hair flying from side to side.

She put her hand gently to the door, then pushed it open with a creak.

"Hey… Are you…here?" she murmured, but there was no response from the dim interior.

She looked around the shed, blinking, then brought her candle inside.

"…?!"

She immediately caught her breath.

There he was, over in a dark corner.

Was he dead or, perhaps, a ghost? The candlelight revealed a seemingly ruined suit of armor. One horn was broken off the steel helmet; the leather armor was grimy, and the wearer had a round shield strapped to one arm and a sword at his hip.

He was crumpled in the corner of the abandoned building. Her heart pounded. She could detect the prickling metallic odor of the steel, mixed with a faint stench. She was used to it from working on the farm: blood and gore.

Cow Girl's expression stiffened. She crouched and approached him, looking him in the face.

"Hey—hey, are you okay?! Did you get hurt?!"

"……"

He gave no answer.

The helmet moved awkwardly, facing toward her. Inside the visor, she thought she could see a red eye.

"No," he said quietly and then slowly stood. "I didn't."

Cow Girl, overwhelmed, fell backward on her bottom. Now she was looking up at him, and in a minor panic, she rushed to cover the front of her shirt. It was a little late for that. Her cheeks burned.

"Er, ah, um…"

"I was merely resting."

The voice sounded faint and strained. Was it because he had just woken up? Cow Girl wondered vacantly.

He picked up a canteen sitting in a corner of the shed and drank emphatically from it. Who knew how long the water had been in there?

Cow Girl, still pressing a hand to the front of her shirt, got unsteadily to her feet.

"Resting? You mean—?"

Here?

The place was in such bad shape it could barely hold off the elements. There was no bed; he was just slumped on the ground.

And he was resting?

"I can sleep even with one eye open."

That wasn't really an answer. At least, not the answer Cow Girl was hoping for.

As she looked on, dumbfounded, he tightened the previously loosened straps of his armor.

"Now I've had my rest."

"You've had…what…?"

She took note of his equipment at a glance: sword, shield, armor, helmet. She didn't know much about adventuring, of course, but even to a layperson like her, it was obvious that he had just gotten back from an adventure and hadn't even changed out of his equipment.

She tried to speak, but her throat constricted. She clenched her hand in front of her generous chest.

"Where…? Where are you going?"

"Goblins." That was all he said. The rattle of his items and equipment sounded in the dim shelter.

Cow Girl realized the candle in her hand had burned out, but she didn't think she could relight it.

Now I see.

With him back, she had selfishly thought that things had started to change. But she was no different than she had been five years ago, and…

…he isn't, either. It's still that *day for him.*

What should she do, then? Cow Girl clenched her fist harder.

His equipment was already settled. All the pieces were there, the straps were fastened, and he was carrying his item bag.

"Ah…" She opened her mouth to say something, but he passed by her at a bold stride without speaking.

She spun around, but he was already out the door, which creaked as he left.

His back was growing farther and farther away. Once again, he was about to go somewhere, alone.

Cow Girl simply couldn't stand the thought. All the muscles in her face worked as she shouted, "I'll be waiting for you!"

A memory broke on her like the dawn.

A childish fight. Tears welling in her eyes, then in his.

Morning. Riding in a carriage, her parents seeing her off. Looking back from her seat. No sign of him.

The words she meant to say to him when she got back. The place she could never return to.

She couldn't go home. She hadn't gone home, and she never would.

No, that wasn't true. She was sick of thinking that way.

"I'll be waiting, so this time—this time—"

I want you to come home.

She didn't know if he heard her or not.

She thought she saw him glance back, but it must have just been her imagination.

Surely, it was a trick of the morning light that made her vision blur, making it impossible to tell.

INTERLUDE
"Sadly, Her Adventure Ended Here"

It happened without a sound, without any sense of anything coming or going. There was only the empty howling of the wind.

Until an instant earlier, Half-Elf Ranger had been there, peppering them with complaints: "It's so damp in here!" "It reeks!"

"Once we take care of these Blobs, we'll go right home," the adventurer assured her, and she had smiled and replied, "Let's give it our all, then."

And then, suddenly, she was gone. Right before their eyes. But to where?

Then one of her boots came down with a thump. Was it from above? Was there something…above them?

There she was.

They could only see her lower body dangling in the hazy dimness.

She was struggling desperately, totally ignoring the fact that one of her boots had fallen off and that her clothes had been hitched up so her underwear was visible.

Her legs, kicking at the air, spasmed each time the party heard the *crunch*, like a chewing sound, until she stopped moving.

Dead? Was she—could she be—dead?

The noises above them continued. There was a clatter, and her bow dropped to the ground in front of them.

She was sucked in, chewed and crushed as she went. Gradually, bit by bit, her legs moved upward and disappeared.

Beside the adventurer, Dwarf Warrior held his battle-ax across his shoulders and cried out.

The monk, a follower of the God of Knowledge, shouted the monster's name.

Plop, plop, plop. Blood, or some other bodily fluid of hers, came spattering down.

It landed on the adventurer's face, something thick and viscous.

There was a creaking crash, as of great teeth gnashing.

It came from a set of giant jaws that belonged to a massive insect, now lowering its head, so large as to fill the whole of their vision.

And from the mouth of the centipede-like beast: blood. Her blood.

"Eee—"

His throat contracted, his tongue nearly stuck; when his voice emerged, it scratched and strained.

"Eeeyaaaaaaaggggghhhhhhh!"

He remembered shouting, running, drawing his sword, and even leaping at the thing.

How he survived—that, he couldn't remember.

The next thing he knew, he was crawling out of there under a twilight sky.

His three—no, two—companions were covered in mud.

The monk had his hand very pointedly on the dwarf's shoulder.

And what about her? He muttered the question in a broken voice, but there was no answer. *We've gotta help...her...* But again, there was no answer.

The monk grabbed him and sent him flying with a punch. He'd had no idea their man of the cloth possessed such strength.

A Rock Eater.

The overzealous mining had chased it out of its habitat. That was why the Blobs had been coming to the surface.

But it wasn't until much later that they would learn any of that.

CHAPTER 5

Advance to the Next Level

Experience and Growth

"What d'you think?" the ugly rhea demanded. "That you're already Little Mister Perfect?" The dim ice cave was deadly cold. "Oh, but you're not. I know: you think you can do anything and everything with exactly what you already have."

The old creature, clad in a mithril shirt, mockingly swung his glinting dagger and spread his arms wide. *"I hate to fail! I never want to lose! And I don't need any special training!"*

His mocking voice echoed, a painful whining sound bouncing off the walls of the cave.

An icicle dangling from the ceiling shattered and then broke away, falling down.

The old man dodged it almost carelessly as it landed at his feet, then picked it up.

"Maybe you've got some astonishing idea in *here* that no one has ever thought of before?"

He brandished the icicle and swung it, breaking it against *his* forehead with a dull crack. Blood welled up, the terrible cold in the room causing it to steam white.

"Don't you get all high and mighty, talking down about others. The lowliest street thug is smarter than you."

The old rhea tossed the icicle aside as if it no longer interested him, then crouched down in a rather unbecoming way.

©Shingo Adachi

"Listen up. I'm gonna teach you that none of that is true."

The boy, now lying on the ground, was unable to answer. He couldn't even sit up.

The reason was that his hands were cruelly bound, and the cold had caused his skin to stick to the ice.

The old man, however, was unbothered by this. He grasped the boy by the head and tore him off the ground.

"You'd better be ready. Understand?"

"Yes," the boy said, finally able to speak. "Master."

"Excellent!" The old rhea grinned broadly and dragged the boy off.

They came to an underground canal—perhaps more of a river—no, perhaps more of a glacier. Snowmelt from the frozen mountain above came down here in a form that just qualified to be called liquid.

Without a word, the rhea pulled the boy over to the frozen stream and then kicked him into it.

"——?!"

His scream never quite took voice. Pain coursed through his body as if every inch of him were being pounded with nails at once. His lungs froze with the cold, his heart felt as if it had been bound and gagged.

He kicked and struggled but only succeeded in sinking. That was when the old man delivered a vicious kick to his head.

"Sink down deep! Then *kick*!" the rhea yowled, gesturing madly with his dagger.

"Do that, and you'll be able to float! Then do it again and again! Otherwise, all that awaits you is death!"

The boy sucked in breath desperately, then sank down. His feet touched ice at the bottom of the channel. He kicked off.

His master was right.

§

Thus, failure became the engine that drove his gradual transformation.

He had traded his round shield for something smaller, removed the handle, and made sure it had a metal rim.

He'd given up on the long sword. He now wore a weapon of an unusual length, several strokes shorter than normal.

His bag of items had moved at some point, from his back to his hip.

His once-untarnished armor had grown covered in mud and blood spatters, becoming utterly grimy.

One of the horns had broken off his steel helmet, which went from cheap-looking to pathetic.

No longer did anyone consider inviting him on adventures.

Goblins, goblins, goblins, goblins, goblins, goblins.

It seemed to be all he ever said, and most other adventurers watched him from a distance and muttered quietly among themselves.

Sometimes, in fact, a bit of discreet betting took place as to who or what was under the armor, and novices who saw him tended to gawk.

No one even attempted to associate with him any longer. Nor did he attempt to associate with anyone.

And yet, so long as one is part of the living world, some bonds, however tenuous, are formed, whether one wants them or not.

§

The first thing the farm owner said to *him* upon opening his mouth was: "You didn't do anything to that girl, did you?"

It was near dawn, the sun still casting purple streaks into the sky. The farm owner stood in front of the shed in the early-morning chill, brandishing a pitchfork.

He was presumably on his way to the Adventurers Guild. He exited the shed and closed the door behind him. Then he faced the owner and said stiffly, "What do you mean by…'anything'?"

"Don't play stupid. You know what I mean."

Several days had passed since that incident.

The farmer was busy with work, but he also cared deeply for his family. He could tell his niece had been deep in thought ever since she had visited the young man's shed that one morning.

She was the last of his family, a priceless memento of the younger sister he had lost, and he treated her like his own daughter.

He knew, of course, that one day she would probably fall in love, marry, and leave his home.

But even so.

"If you have, well—I assume you're ready and willing to take responsibility." The farmer spoke in a low voice, almost a growl, and stared intently at the young man.

It was impossible to say what he was thinking under that literally expressionless steel face.

If the boy was trying to take advantage of her in any way, the farmer would give him something to think about with the pitchfork in his hand. That much, he felt, was his right as her adoptive parent and guardian.

"No." The helmet shook back and forth. "I didn't do anything in particular."

The voice was low and nonchalant, and so frank as to take the wind out of the farmer's sails. If the words were a lie, then this young man was a reprobate quite accustomed to the act.

The farmer stared at the steel helmet a moment longer, then finally looked away as if suddenly unsure where to put his eyes. "Is that so?"

"Yes."

A rooster crowed in the distance. The sun would be fully risen soon, and the day would start. The farmer squinted against the brightness and heaved a sigh.

"You have no intention of taking up an honorable occupation?"

He meant to imply that he would never give his niece to some goon of an adventurer.

But then, too, if she could live decently with a survivor from her village, that would be ideal.

At the very least—yes, at the very least, the farmer finally realized, blinking. He discovered he had admitted how serious the young man was—so much so that he had been prepared to forgive him with just a bit of a pitchfork thrashing.

But then, the young man said, "No," and shook his head firmly. "Because there are goblins."

"..."

And then this. The farmer didn't speak. He quickly began to regret his overeager resolution. He'd thought his niece had begun to recover over these last five years; no wonder she was upset now.

"Well, you'd better get going, then. Got to get to work."

This man is completely gone already...

That much was obvious, not least because he appeared to have just crawled through a pool of mud.

As the farm owner started to walk away, pitchfork in his hand and his mind swirling with bitter thoughts, he heard the young man say, "Yes," from behind him.

Then came a question: "...Where is she?"

This caused the farmer to stop and raise an eyebrow.

Here he had thought the young man was completely uninterested in her.

He turned around to find the young man standing almost as if bored.

"She's gone out. Don't think she'll be back till late today."

"Is that so," murmured the young man, and then he set off toward town at a shuffle. There was something doubt-filled in his gait; to the farmer, he somehow looked like a child who had been left all alone.

§

"Ah...!"

When Guild Girl finally looked up from the desk she had stretched herself out on, the morning rush had already begun.

She heard the door open, and then a bold, almost violent, but casual set of footsteps made its way over to her.

"Goblins."

No one looked up any longer when that word sounded from the reception desk. When the looming adventurer with his grimy equipment showed up, everyone pretended they had something else that demanded their attention.

And who could blame them? Everyone knew that *he* was not quite all there.

Whether it was fate or destiny that controlled the world, adventurers were a superstitious lot. Avoiding any involvement with "strange types" was a form of self-preservation.

But none of that mattered to Guild Girl. She got a bright smile on her face and held out some paperwork she had already prepared.

They were, of course, goblin-slaying quests.

I don't like the feeling that I'm sort of foisting these on him, but…

She ignored the prickle in her heart. Somebody had to do this work. Mid-level adventurers flatly refused, and even beginners wouldn't always take these jobs. Who was left to help the people in need?

Not that the work everyone else does isn't important, too.

Hence, she gave him the leftovers. Adventurers who came in early in the morning picked over the quests that had been put out, and this was what was left.

This way, she could assign goblin slaying without causing anyone any trouble (*trouble?*).

"Ahem, we have five cases today. Everyone else just now is off dealing with a commotion at the mines…"

Guild Girl flipped through one page and then another, careful to remain polite as she went through the explanation. She used to stutter and hesitate, but not anymore—at least, not often. And that, too, was thanks to him.

It wasn't that she considered her interactions with him to be practice, or that she thought of him as someone to practice upon, but…

"…?"

Guild Girl paused, looking at him in perplexity. He neither responded, nor questioned her about anything.

There in front of her was the cheap-looking helmet she had grown so accustomed to. It leaned slightly to one side—maybe because the horn on the other side was broken off—but that was one of the things she found endearing about him.

She thought, just maybe, she saw the helmet shake listlessly from side to side.

"Er… Are you feeling poorly?"

"…" He was silent for a second but then said, "No," with an awkward shake of his head. "I'm fine," he added.

Hmm, Guild Girl muttered to herself. It wasn't at all clear to her what was "fine."

I wish I could at least see his face.

As the thought crossed her mind, she realized that the only time she had gotten a clear look at him was back when he had first registered.

Now she wished she had looked closer at the time, but it was too late for that now.

"..."

Silence.

Guild Girl gave a delicate cough.

"Pardon me," she said, tapping a finger on the counter. The smile remained pasted on her face. Staring down the unreadable steel helmet, she found herself growing unaccountably angry. "Do you think I can entrust work like this to someone in such bad shape that he can barely stand up?"

"I'm fine."

The repeated response provoked a slam of Guild Girl's fist upon the desk. Her colleague shot her a piercing glance, but Guild Girl ignored her. The words were out of her mouth now, and she was on the warpath.

"Do you really think that?" Still smiling, she leaned over until her face was inches from his.

She thought she heard a mumble from inside the helmet, and finally the word *no* emerged clearly.

"Proper rest is essential for safe adventuring!" *No rest, no quests*, she told him, and was pleased to see him nod slightly in return.

"Very well."

Ha! How about that? Guild Girl sat up a little straighter, feeling the flush of triumph.

Maybe I'll cut him a break now, she thought and softened her voice as she said, "Okay, then. Just this once... I'll give you this."

She reached behind the counter and picked out one of the pieces of merchandise the Guild kept there. It was a faintly colored liquid in a bottle. A stamina potion.

It was not, of course, permitted to give such things away to adventurers. That would cut into the Guild's all-important profits. But the solution was simple enough: Guild Girl would pay for it later out of her own salary. That would make things even, she figured.

"Our little secret, okay?" She winked at him.

From deep in the helmet, there was an *erk* sound, and then he said, "...Sorry."

"The expression is *thank you*," she replied. "If you really want those brownie points." She giggled. "On that note. There are five cases here, but…all the other adventurers are out…"

"Out?" he asked, his voice especially low.

"Hmm?" Guild Girl said, cocking her head before nodding. "Yes."

Now, that's a little odd…

If she wasn't just imagining it, his voice sounded…genuinely angry.

"Yes. To the mines. There was a fairly serious incident there. Would you rather join them?"

"No." He shook his head, then took one of the quest papers. "I will slay goblins."

"That one is—"

Guild Girl skimmed the paper afresh. It was a quest from a pioneer village on the frontier. *Goblin trouble. Please get rid of them.* A perfectly ordinary quest.

The numbers are unusually high, though…

The number of goblins people claimed to have seen bothered her.

"You're…sure you'll be all right?"

Guild Girl tried to ask a lot in a few words. His health. The fact that he was working solo.

An ugly premonition that this might be the one he didn't come back from whispered through her mind. She suddenly discovered a deep ache in her chest, and without really meaning to, she leaned closer to him.

"I'm… I'm sure if you wait awhile, some other adventurers will show up…"

"These goblins," he said in a clipped tone. "I will face them alone."

§

"You again, huh?" The workshop boss looked up and frowned, his foot pausing on his treadle grindstone.

Keeping a sword sharp required this sort of thing be done constantly. The blade was placed against a spinning grindstone, sending sparks flying. Sharpening a sword involved literally shaving away part of the blade. Eventually it would reach its limit.

Some enchanted blades and magical items might be exceptions, but otherwise, the item's ultimate destruction was inevitable. Even elves, proverbially ageless, could not escape the perpetual flow of time.

But even so…

The boss's eyes went wide when he picked up the sword that the strange-looking man had brought him. The man had placed it on the boss's countertop, and it was not in good shape.

It wasn't so much that the sword had been shorn down to a strange length. There was a more fundamental problem.

It was badly chipped, covered in fat and blood. It could practically have passed for a saw, and he had seen meat cleavers in a cleaner state than this.

As if that weren't enough, the hilt was bent as if it had been used to strike something, while the pommel was nearly shattered.

"Feh. Those who don't look after their equipment are never long for this world."

"I don't believe I'm not looking after my equipment."

The quiet voice drew an exasperated "Is that what y'really think?" from the boss.

Common wisdom holds that a single sword can cut down five enemies. An amateur eager to show how smart he is might argue that this is untrue, just a bit of folk wisdom. But needless to say, it is the former who is correct and the latter who is mistaken.

You might think this makes a certain sense: a master swordsman can judge the condition of his blade, keep it from getting damaged, and prevent gore from sticking to it.

And yet, when is a sword used but in the heat of battle? There is armor and skin. Sometimes, a weapon may strike bone or be used recklessly. If one of those wayward blows lands on enemy armor, a sword may be damaged. As it cuts through blood vessels, a sword may become covered in viscera.

Further, the hilt and pommel make excellent impromptu war hammers.

A single sword can cut down five enemies.

For most people. But this guy…?

The boss ran a finger along the blade, giving a disappointed shake of his head.

"This thing's beyond a little polishing. I'll take it off you. Buy a new one instead."

"Understood."

The boss tossed the sword into a basket of pig iron, then told the young man how much it would be to exchange.

Without hesitation, the adventurer took his purse from his item bag and slapped a coin on the countertop. To all appearances, the purse looked quite heavy.

"Well, well, making quite a living. What is it you're doing?"

"Slaying goblins."

"Hrm?" The boss squeezed one eye shut and gave him a suspicious look. "So you and your party have a common fund for equipment, then?"

"I'm solo."

This provoked a deep groan from the workshop boss.

In other words, this man had to cut down far more than five enemies with a single sword. It wouldn't hurt him to use something of a slightly higher quality...

"Have you finished what I asked for?"

"Sure have."

Nah. He would keep that thought to himself.

The boss passed the young man a new sword, scabbard and all, and the adventurer secured it at his hip. The boss gave a shake of his head. He reached behind the counter and took out a package covered in oil paper, unwrapping it with his thick fingers.

There was a soft clinking sound as an overshirt of fine mail spilled out on the counter. But he had oiled it carefully; compared to the cacophony of plate metal, this was hardly a whisper. It could be worn under the young man's leather armor and still allow him to sneak about while providing adequate defense.

The eyes of the links, though, were on the large side; a thin enough sword could stab through them. This was no mithril shirt, just finely worked wire.

Nonetheless, it was a big step up from having nothing. It was more than enough to save a life.

"It ain't the best stuff around," the boss said.

But it should be enough to meet his requirements. The boss gazed at the visor of the steel helmet.

The voice that replied was, as always, diffident and quiet. "I know," he said. "It's not a problem."

"What's not a problem?"

"It won't be a big deal if a goblin uses it."

In other words, if a goblin steals it, eh?

Adventurers possessed thin swords. Thin enough that they could stab a goblin wearing this shirt.

The boss saw that this was the basis on which the adventurer was choosing his equipment: what might happen if it was taken by goblins. And it wasn't lost on him what that meant.

§

"I need provisions."

"Sure thing! How many days' worth?"

"One week."

"Coming right up!"

Padfoot Waitress bounded off. *He* ignored her and looked around.

He was in the Adventurers Guild tavern. He hardly ever came here, except when buying provisions. He was such a rare visitor, in fact, that he had only just now discovered that the place had a padfoot server.

One thing he did notice was that in the middle of the day like this, the tavern had a lethargic air about it. The adventurers who were seated here and there around the room were either on a day off or had gotten back early from some excursion. Some nursed drinks, while others listlessly munched snack foods, but none of them looked inspired by their activities.

One person among them stood out to him.

"...Damn it all... What the hell...? Argh...!"

He recognized the adventurer who leaned over one of the tables, muttering to himself. It was the young man he had encountered on that goblin-slaying quest, the one who had registered the same day he had.

There was no sign of his party around, and the adventurer himself appeared thoroughly drunk. No one else in the bar looked at him; everyone seemed to be consciously avoiding contact.

He thought for a moment, then kept silent and waited for his provisions to come. Even he realized there were times when people just wanted to be left alone.

But knowing was one thing…

"Hey there. What's up? Heading off on an adventure?"

…and being left alone was another. Somebody sat down heavily across from him as he waited.

He looked up and saw a tall, handsome, muscular man. He wore leather armor and carried a spear across his back. The grin this person leveled at him was less friendly than it was vaguely triumphant.

"What's on the menu for you? Giant centipedes? Ghouls?"

A little dungeon-dive wouldn't go amiss, either.

He, however, only stared at the jabbering spear wielder, before finally replying, "Goblins."

"Guh! Goblins?!" Spearman said with exaggerated drama. His eyes went wide, and he tossed his shoulders back, his mouth open as if aghast. "Me, I was in the mines the other day clearing out Blobs!"

"Is that so?"

"Damn right it is! Pretty impressive, huh!"

He, however, had no idea what a Blob was. A moment's reflection led him to the conclusion that it was not a goblin.

"Is that impressive?"

"Damn right!"

"I see." He nodded. "I'm impressed."

"What're you, makin' fun of me?!" This time, Spearman leaned forward as if to grab him, his face contorted in anger.

He was silent in thought for a moment, then tilted his steel helmet gently. "Then is it not impressive?"

"Aw, fer—! Dammit, what is it with this guy?!"

Spearman was very outgoing and very loud. He shouted in frustration, then slumped back in his chair as if to say, *I give up*. The back of the chair creaked under his enthusiastic display of distress.

Spearman pursed his lips in dissatisfaction, then picked up his beloved spear and started spinning it around playfully. Suddenly, his eyes narrowed, and he pointed to the bag at *his* hip.

"Hey, what's that?"

As a matter of fact, there was a bottle poking out from the mouth of the young man's item pouch. He must have forgotten to close it. Nothing more than simple carelessness. He gave a click of his tongue.

"It's a stamina potion." He took out the bottle, rearranged the contents of his item pouch, and stuffed the bottle back in. Now there was no danger of dropping it. "I received it at the reception desk."

"Whaaaat?!" Spearman threw himself forward again. His shouting reverberated inside the steel helmet. "Damn! I need to put my best foot forward with Guild Girl... Blob slaying!"

"Blobs."

"Yeah, they're hunks of living liquid. You can't tell where to stab 'em! So I took my spear and—"

"Right, then... That's, enough...already."

Spearman's tale of martial valor was interrupted by a beautiful, buxom woman, whose hips swayed as she came over to the table and sat down. Her clothes accented the lines of her body, and she wore a distinctive hat: she was clearly a witch.

"You oughta get in on this. Those blobs weren't nice to you, neith— Owwww!"

Looking entirely disinterested, the woman brought her staff down on Spearman's head. She checked to see that he was safely unconscious, then gave a small sigh.

"Sorry, about, him." She gave a flirtatious glance.

He shook his head. "It was no problem."

"One of these days...I'll use Spider Web or, something, to shut him...up."

"I see." He nodded. Then, as if the thought had just crossed his mind, he directed his gaze toward the drunken adventurer he had seen earlier. "What happened to him?"

"Ah..." Witch let her eyes with their long eyelashes drift shut slightly, running her tongue along her luscious lips wistfully. "One, was, eaten. Another, went to deliver, her effects. The third, his arm... well."

He left the party after that. Witch didn't sound especially interested in any of this. She produced a pipe from somewhere mysterious, using a flint to light it—*click*—with an experienced hand.

She drew in a long, lazy breath, sweet-smelling smoke wafting into the air around her.

"There's just one left. All common, enough... Don't you think?"

"...I see."

"And that's, the story. See you..."

Witch gave a quick wave and grabbed Spearman by the collar. Spearman mumbled something about the unfairness of it all, but he didn't resist as Witch dragged him away.

She was either quite strong for someone who stood on the back row, or perhaps she and Spearman were somehow involved with each other.

After a moment, he decided he didn't care either way and chased the thought from his head.

"Sorry to keep you waiting!"

Padfoot Waitress came bounding back out of the kitchen with impeccable timing. She took the seven packs of rations clutched to her chest and dumped them on the table.

He checked them over and then shoved them into his item pouch, setting down several silver coins from his purse in return.

"Thank you! A pleasure doing business with you!"

His bag was starting to bulge. He adjusted some items to make room for the provisions, then strode away.

He had one hand on the door when he stopped and looked back. The adventurer he had noticed earlier gave him a vacant stare.

He looked at the other man for a moment, then he pushed open the door and went outside.

The door opened and shut with a creaking sound that stayed in his ears for an unusually long time.

§

Wssh. Wssh wssh. The wind blew gently through the underbrush, making a sound like waves on the shore.

There was nothing there. Just a path, completely unremarkable, like any of a thousand other paths anywhere.

Cow Girl held back her hair against the wind, squinting her eyes. She could see the scorched timbers poking up out of the emerald sea.

"Here we go. Right where the quest specified, Miss." The speaker was an adventurer with a spear at his side, sitting in the driver's seat of the carriage they had rented.

"Mm. Thank you…"

She bowed her head from her perch on the luggage rack, eliciting a smile from the spearman's witch companion. Witch didn't look to be that much older than Cow Girl, but she gave off a very womanly air.

"Well, then. We'll, be right…here, waiting for you."

"Okay."

She thanked them again and then jumped down from the carriage. The grass underfoot when she landed nearly cost her her footing, but she quickly caught herself.

"You okay there?" Spearman asked.

"Fine, thanks," Cow Girl said.

You'd think I would remember this place.

In another carriage, on another day, she had seen this same spot growing smaller in the distance.

She was in the same place, looking the same direction.

There's nothing here.

Only the wind rustling in the grass. Cow Girl started walking slowly.

She always used to play on this road. Until five years ago, she had used it every day.

The look of the place, still fresh in her memory, clashed with what she saw before her. It made her feel almost dizzy, and she found her footsteps light and uncertain.

"…Hmm."

Pushing through the crackling underbrush, Cow Girl headed for her destination. It was very subtle, but close attention revealed a spot where the grass cover was just a little thinner than elsewhere. That showed where the road used to be.

Finally, she arrived at a spreading, grassy plain. As expected, there was nothing there. Just a few carbonized pillars, buried in the vegetation.

Cow Girl stepped reverently into the grassy square. The crunch under her boots came, perhaps, from the last remnants of old flagstones.

What happened to all of this?

Her father. Her mother.

Her favorite outfit. The doll she had loved. The bed she had slept in every night. Her special eating utensils.

All of it, gone.

Cow Girl stood gazing at nothing before she was finally able to look around.

Hardly anyone must have remembered that there was once a village here.

Just her, and her uncle, and *him*.

All of it was in the past now.

To think, this was what had happened in just five years. In ten or twenty—every trace would surely vanish.

Nobody likes where they are...

The muscles of her face twitched, almost a grimace; she flopped down on her back to distract herself. She felt the grass against her back and neck, oddly ticklish.

In the distance, Spearman called out in alarm, followed by Witch hushing him in a quieter voice.

The sky above her was almost absurdly blue, and the white of the clouds filled her eyes.

"...That's it, isn't it?"

Cow Girl couldn't spend every minute mourning. She had to eat her food and do her work. She wanted to laugh and enjoy herself.

That was perfectly normal—who could begrudge her that or mock her for it?

Similar things had happened all over the world.

She blinked her eyes, too full of light, and then put her arm over her face to block out the sun.

It would be so simple, feel so good, just to throw everything away and lose herself in grief.

But I absolutely can't do that.

Without the sunlight to fill her vision, the image of *him* in the corner of that shed floated into her mind.

I really can't, can I?

Then, what could she do?

What could she do for him?

What action should she take?

"...Okay!"

Cow Girl gave a great kick, using the momentum to pull herself to her feet. She patted her backside to brush off the dust and grass, then gave herself an invigorating smack on both cheeks. She would just have to summon all her energy and throw herself into it.

She headed back to the carriage at a quick clip. Witch saw her coming and put a hand to the brim of her hat.

"Done, al...ready?"

"Yep!" Cow Girl nodded energetically, bouncing up onto the carriage. The wood protested faintly. She bowed to both of the adventurers. "Sorry for dragging you out here..."

"Heck, work is work," the spear-wielding adventurer said with a friendly laugh. "We do whatever we're asked, as long as we get paid. So no worries."

"Work..."

I wonder if he *thinks of what he does as work. And if so...first, he has to finish it.*

Cow Girl clenched her fist. Witch chuckled as if this amused her.

"Perhaps, you...should cut your, hair."

"Huh?"

She hadn't expected this. Her eyes widened. Witch brushed a pale finger over Cow Girl's bangs.

"Cut, it. To show your, eyes. Don't you think, you'd be...cute that, way?"

I wonder...

Cow Girl took a lock of her own hair in her hands, considering the idea.

Spearman gave a shout, and the carriage clattered off.

§

Should I have taken a carriage?

It was an uncharacteristic thought for *him*. He stopped walking.

The sun was past its peak already and was beginning to work its way down through the sky. A good deal of light still fell on the path, but soon enough, all would be covered in darkness.

If he was going to consider camping for the night, he would have to make preparations soon.

"..."

I was late setting out.

If he had left first thing in the morning, he would surely have been at the village by now.

Roadways often had inns or other accommodations along them—but only if you were going somewhere anybody cared about.

A near–ghost town on the frontier was not such a place.

If he walked through the night, he could presumably reach the village, but when he thought about having to fight goblins immediately after that...

The thought, though, was not what counted in this case. He could stand still, but the sun would not; he had to act.

He looked this way and that around the reedy fields nearby, until he found what he was looking for. He waded into the grasses, causing them to whish.

He had discovered the remains of some town or city. Had this area been a battlefield back in the Age of the Gods? Or was this simply a ruined village?

The rotted-out shells of houses dotted the landscape, almost as if sleeping among the weeds. He located a stone wall that had retained roughly its original shape, but when he gave it a firm kick, it came tumbling down. So did several other walls, but finally, he found one that survived his abuse.

This is a good spot.

Several blows showed no sign of knocking the barrier down, so he settled in front of it, spreading a waterproof cloth on the ground. There was no need to let the night dew chill him, inhibiting his ability to regain his stamina. That would serve no purpose.

He unhitched his sword from his hip, using it in lieu of a hatchet to cut some of the brush, making a space for a fire. If he were to start a fire that then spread to the grass around him, causing him to die of smoke inhalation—well, there could be no stupider way to go.

Next, procure fuel. This wasn't especially difficult. He just needed to collect some dry grass. If only living wood was available, it would be simple enough to dry out as he went along.

He took stones from the shattered buildings to build a little pit that would keep the wind at bay and the fire contained, and he put the fuel in it.

Finally, he only had to light a bit of grass as a fire starter and toss it down inside. Then he was done.

"..."

He was silent, and he didn't light the fire just yet.

The sky above him was blue. No dark clouds on the horizon, and the air was dry: it wasn't likely to rain. No need for a roof, then, he figured; he simply put his back to the wall and sat down.

Everything around him was as silent as the grave. The clouds passed overhead without a sound; the only noise was the susurrus of the grass that came up with every breath of wind.

He took a waterskin from his pouch, unstoppering it and taking one, then two big mouthfuls. He was surprised at the wave of fatigue that assaulted him when he sat down. His eyelids were terribly heavy.

He couldn't rest now, though. If he didn't have a fire going at night, he might wake to find some wild animal gnawing on him.

He set the waterskin to one side, then took out a hunk of dried meat from his pouch and inserted it through the visor of his helmet. Each time he chewed the tough stuff, a burst of salt filled his mouth. He had been hoping that working his jaws would be enough to ward off the sleepiness, but he was also pleased to find the food did not taste as bad as he had expected.

"..."

When he looked at the wrapper around the meat, he saw a familiar symbol. It had come from the farm.

He chewed the meat silently, interspersed with an occasional sip of water, sitting still there in the shade. The light of summer seemed to fill his whole helmet, leaving him with a dull ache in his head. It was because of the heat.

Ever aware of the possibility of a goblin sneak attack, he pushed away the impulse to take off his headgear.

Thus, he waited as the sun gradually went down.

At length, the field on the distant horizon turned crimson with twilight, the stars and the twin moons rising to replace the sun in the sky. One of the moons was red, as if aflame, while the green moon seemed chill, cold. He stared at them up in the sky.

It was his older sister, so far as he recalled, who had taught him to connect the stars into pictures of heroes.

Now's about the right time.

He struck a flint, the sparks cascading into the fire pit and summoning forth little licking tongues of flame. A thin plume of white smoke rose directly up into the sky.

"..."

This would probably be enough to keep away the animals. But as for goblins? He wasn't sure. Would they come? Perhaps so.

They did not fear fire. Maybe they didn't even realize that most living beings did.

They had, in fact, come, once. That, he must not forget. A voice echoed around in his head. Someone's voice.

His throat was agonizingly dry. He tried licking his lips, but it wasn't enough to take his mind off it. Well, he would arrive at the village the next day. He picked up his waterskin and drank greedily, the liquid sloshing over the sides of his helmet.

What was in the pouch, in fact, was a thin grape wine. Not that he was particularly interested in either the flavor or the alcoholic content.

At last, he closed one eye, leaving the other open to peer into the night. In his right hand, he grasped his sword, his knees up against his chest so he could get to his feet at any time.

With his one open eye, he thought he saw something at the edges of the flickering shadows of the fire.

"...!"

He brought up his sword, slicing through the air. With another breath, he sheathed the sword, then drew it again.

Goblin skulls he would smash, their throats he would pierce. Pierce and smash. Stop their breath. Permanently.

And thus, he waited until dawn for goblins to appear.

But none ever did.

CHAPTER 6

SOLO ADVENTURE

Not Even Seven Adventurers

Her teacher told her not to go outside that day, but her curiosity was more persuasive than her instructor.

There was a part of the temple's outer wall that was broken, and this would be an excellent opportunity to see if she could get out via the gap.

"Hrrn…ahh… There! Heh-heh! Nothing to it."

Her clothes were covered in dust, but she paid the fact no mind as she made a sound of triumph and stuck out her as yet undeveloped chest.

Beyond the hole was a field of grass and a blue sky. Piercingly bright sunlight announced that summer would soon arrive.

The girl had long, black hair that stuck out every which way. Her tunic, tied with a belt, had patches all over it and, now, dirt, too.

She gave her clothes a brisk dusting off, and then started running, dragging her feet in her big, ill-fitting sandals.

She was heading for the village gate, which was connected to Outside by a road. Not that she had any idea what was actually out there.

I sure hope I don't miss them!

She ran up to the fence and around, but she didn't see anyone. *Thank goodness, I'm in time.* She sat herself down on the fence. She kicked her legs, scratching her toenails against her sandals. There was a gentle breeze that felt wonderful against her sweating, overheated limbs.

Maybe I'll go swimming in the river later.

Teacher didn't let them play outside very much these days, and the girl didn't like it. Her teacher had always been given to little nagging aphorisms—"Better to study than play" chief among them—but recently, it had been especially bad.

Goblins were about, she said. She wouldn't tell them whether there was a nest nearby; maybe she didn't know herself. If she didn't know, why didn't she just say so?

She probably thinks that if she told me there was a nest, I'd go look for it.

But the girl was hardly stupid enough to do such a thing by herself. She would need at least two or three of her friends from the Temple to join in.

"Yawn... Ahh... Hmm..."

As this nonsense passed through her head, she soon found herself yawning. The early summer sun was perfect for a little nap. She would wait just a little longer, and then if the person she was expecting didn't show up, she would just close her eyes for a few minutes.

"But then..."

If she had run away just to sleep and play, what would she say when Teacher gave her the inevitable scolding? *But I was going to*—she would say, but her reason for slipping away would have vanished.

"Maybe I could say a little kid was crying, so I went and got some fruit for them? Nah, used that one already..."

Hmm. She crossed her arms thoughtfully, until she found herself leaning backward so far that she could see behind herself.

"Whoops!" She wheeled her arms, trying to balance herself, until she landed on the ground with a little thump. It was an excellent landing, even by her standards, and she allowed herself a satisfied smile. No one else at the temple school could do the same.

It's pretty simple, though... The words left her mouth in a mutter. That was when she noticed the dark figure in the distance. It was striding along the road, coming straight at her. A man.

"Is this the village where the goblins appeared?"

"Yup!" she replied, feigning indifference. But then she cocked her head in his direction: "Hmm?"

©Shingo Adachi

For the first time, she took a good look at him from head to toe and was perplexed by what she saw. "You're dressed weird…"

"Is that so?"

Grimy leather armor, a cheap-looking steel helmet with one horn broken off. At his hip, a sword of a strange length. On his arm was a small, round shield.

He was the first adventurer the ten-year-old girl had ever seen.

§

"Gods above! And after I told you all those times not to go outside!"

"But I thought… I thought maybe I should help the adventurer get around the village…"

"This village is too small for him to need any help!"

The girl's crying echoed around the temple. She had received her share of whacks to the head.

"Just go back to your room," the teacher said. The girl nodded weakly, and the instructor shooed her away. Then she cleared her throat. "I'm very sorry you had to see that…"

"Not at all," *he* said with a shake of his head. "She did show me here."

"It's kind of you to say that. That girl is certainly energetic, if nothing else."

The instructor of the temple school was a woman with a stern face, no longer young; but when she looked at the children, her eyes softened.

He saw the windmill, the symbol of the God of Trade. This deity oversaw travelers and fortune, as well as merchantry. In addition, he was the god of the ties that bind. Perhaps it was only natural that his temple should take in orphans, but this woman looked especially qualified to run a school like this.

"A battle claimed her parents, but she hasn't become bitter. She helps around the temple whenever she can."

"Is that so?"

"If those children were to lose their homes again, to some monsters…"

"..."

He was quiet, pondering, then he nodded. "I have my intention."

The instructor seemed to take this answer as encouraging. A question formed in her mind. Without losing her smile, she said, "And where might your companions be?"

"..."

He gave no answer but simply stood there, staring straight ahead.

Actually, she didn't know if he was staring. It was impossible to see inside that helmet.

"Hello?" the instructor said dubiously, and the helmet stirred as if he were just now noticing her.

"What?"

"Oh, no, I simply...wondered about your other party members. If they—"

"No."

"You mean they're coming later?"

"I'm solo."

That caused the teacher's eyes to go wide.

No sooner had he made this brusque comment than he reached into his item pouch and drew out his purse. He pulled a silver coin from it and held it out.

"This should cover my room. I may need your help with other things, as well."

"G-goodness..."

Even the Guild had not entirely settled questions of this nature. The quest filers were offering a reward, so they shouldn't be required to furnish room and board as well. On the other hand, should adventurers have to pay to stay wherever a particular quest was located?

It would be simple enough to include room and board in the reward, but since the reward by definition was provided upon successful completion of the quest, it was impossible to pay in advance.

On the other hand, if these expenses were considered entirely the responsibility of the quest filer, there were adventurers who would take a quest, accept a free meal, and then simply leave.

By long-standing custom, therefore, exact payment for lodging and food was settled by negotiation between the adventurer and his hosts.

"Well, thank you very much."

Having said all that, this was the temple of the God of Trade. Clerics couldn't live on thin air, and neither could the orphaned children. The abbess took the coin with an experienced hand, scratching the edge with one nail. "Our gratitude for this blessing," she said firmly and then dropped the coin in her pocket. "You'll have to excuse me," she added. "So many coins of poor quality circulating these days." Smiling sweetly, she said, "May the god's wrath be on all their heads."

"So," he said calmly, nonchalantly. His voice was like a rumble in the earth. "Where are the goblins?"

§

The village was a small pioneer settlement at the foot of a mountain, just a dozen houses or so huddled up against a hill. The sort of tiny village you might find anywhere.

There were no old ruins for them to take advantage of, no highway running through town. It was just a speck of a place where people tried to farm and canvass the mountains enough to earn something to live on.

One man, an adventurer, strode boldly through the village. He looked strange and unusual, and the people watched him at a cautious distance.

"Hey, is that the adventurer they were talking about?"

"I hear he's a warrior. Ain't no novice, judging by that armor."

"How d'you know? He might've just filched it off some battlefield."

"Just the one of him, though? I thought adventurers usually traveled in packs of five or six."

"I hope he won't come to grief like that..."

"It ain't—*you* know. He ain't gonna try to put this on us, is he? Turn us into a fighting force or something?"

"Who knows?"

The gist of the whispered conversations was not very favorable to the adventurer. Maybe that was only to be expected. The villagers had known that they were likely to get amateurs, but they had expected a full party of five or six people, including a scout and a warrior.

Instead, they had gotten this one swordsman in beat-up gear, and they couldn't quite believe it.

It was just as much to be expected that they would follow the adventurer on his rounds when he said he wanted to start by having a look around the village.

He suddenly stopped walking when he had done a single circuit all the way around the village, following the fence that ran around the settlement.

"So the mountain is to the north," he murmured, quietly enough that the villagers were unsure whether he was talking to himself or asking them.

The villagers all looked at one another until someone, somewhere in the crowd, muttered, "That's right."

He fell silent again at that.

At length, the person unfortunate enough to be closest to him ventured a question: "What 'bout it?"

"How steep is it?" he asked.

"G-gentle enough for a horse, I s'pose."

"Any caves or the like?"

"Not sure myself, but we have a woodsman. You could ask him."

"I'd like to."

The villager set off at a gentle jog. Still standing there, *he* grunted softly.

They claimed they didn't know where the goblins were attacking from. Just that every night, the creatures slipped past the guards and over the fence, running roughshod over the fields before they fled.

At first, the villagers suspected it might just be bandits. But that idea was disproved by the discovery of obviously nonhuman footprints.

How many were there? The villagers could only say, "a lot."

In other words, it was the same way such quests usually ended up at the Guild.

After a few minutes, the villager came jogging back. "I asked him, and he said there ain't no grottos nor old ruins."

"I see," the adventurer said, nodding thoughtfully. "Wanderers, then."

They had been chased out of wherever they had been living before and were looking for a new home. They had settled on this village as a place where they could get food, as well as women, both to help them pass the time and furnish them with new goblins.

In any event, they couldn't be left alone. That was why he was here.

"I have a request, if you don't mind."

"Heh?"

"I will pay you. I need the leftover wood from the building of this fence, as well as some carpentry tools." He took several silver coins out of his purse and gave them to the villager.

"That's well and good, but these coins…they ain't been shaved down, have they?"

"I received them as a reward payment from the Guild," he said flatly, even as the villager ran a nail along the coin and gave it a dubious look.

"I guess that's fine, then," the villager said and slipped the coin into a patchwork pocket.

Shaving down the edge of a coin, thereby reducing the weight, and saving the filings was a common way of "saving money." It was, of course, illegal, as it reduced the value of the currency, but there was no end of those who tried it anyway. If he had been a common tough and not an adventurer, the villager might have pressed him harder on the point. As it was, it was hardly surprising that the man should regard this strangely: the adventurer was supposedly here to make money, yet here he was paying to slay goblins!

"Thank ya, I'll be right back with the materials."

"Do you post guards at night?"

"We have some of the young men keep watch."

In place of the man who had gone to fulfill the adventurer's request, this answer came from an older man who seemed likely to be the village chief.

"Not all of 'em, though," he went on. "The duty rotates…"

"Keep doing it. We don't want the goblins to know anything has changed."

"Yessir," the headman said with a nod. He couldn't quite hide the hint of doubt in his voice, but his expression had softened immensely after seeing that silver coin change hands. A person willing to pay his own way was one who had earned a certain amount of trust.

"I'm going to prepare."

"Prepare?"

"Yes." The adventurer nodded, looking intently all around the village.

He thought chances were good that the goblins would come from the mountain to the rear. But that was no reason not to be wary of the other three directions.

Farmers' fields were usually split into three: one sown in spring, one in autumn, and one left to lie fallow. The crops in spring fields had not quite begun to grow yet, but those planted in autumn were near to harvest. When he saw the ripe cabbages and turnips, and the bobbing wheat and beanstalks, he knew what the goblins would be after.

The fallow fields posed a danger of their own. Currently, only white clover, food for the livestock, grew there, and getting into the fields was easy. For the time being, the goblins were contenting themselves with stealing vegetables, but soon enough, they would move on to animals, and then village girls.

They didn't have the luxury of time. But could they gain a little?

"Would it be possible to bring in the harvest early?"

"I guess we could do that." The headman turned sun-scorched, dejected eyes toward the fields, blinking against the brightness. "If we start now, with everyone pitching in at a good pace, we might be done by tomorrow noon."

"Do that, then."

His words caused the village chief to start waving his bony arms, giving instructions to the hovering villagers. Several men and women hurried to grab tools from a shed, then headed for the fields.

He didn't know whether the individual farmers owned the fields, or if the village had serfs. Whatever the case, though, it would be better for the villagers to harvest slightly before things were ripe rather than to have all of it stolen from them. Even if those people were serfs, they would presumably be eager to harvest.

"That's where you draw your water from, isn't it?" he asked, turning his eyes to the river that flowed past the village. It was a shallow thing, not enough to be an obstacle to a goblin despite their short stature.

The problem was the irrigation canals that connected the river to the town.

"Raise the volume of water in the canals. I want to use them as a moat."

At this, the headman raised an eyebrow.

"I assume the canals are deep enough that a child could drown in one."

"Er, yes, well, it's technically the local lord who owns the water..." He glanced at a water mill standing along the river. It bore the insignia of the governor; there was no other building in the area large enough to mill flour.

In other words, the river's current belonged to the governor, too, and if they wanted to use it, they would have to pay taxes. Since they were paying taxes, the governor would like to protect the area; that he was unable to do so showed how difficult things were on the frontier. They couldn't expect the military to intervene against mere goblins. Even on the off chance they did, how many days would it take just to muster the men?

"It's rained of late, so the river's running high."

Farmers are clever people, though, and they do what they can to get by. *He* knew that very well. He came from a village himself, after all—although not this one.

Beneath his helmet, he closed his eyes to steady his shaking vision and swirling thoughts. He took one deep breath.

If he were a goblin, what would he do? What would he aim for? What would he resent?

If you resent someone, you become a goblin.

It was true; he was sure of it.

"Also, prepare for a festival."

"A festival?"

"Yes." He nodded. "I hate to say it, but we must let the creatures do as they will tonight. Tomorrow night, however, it will be different." With a growl, he looked around the village one more time.

What should one do, when one could be attacked from any direction?

"First, spikes."

In fact, there was a great deal he needed to attend to.

§

"All right—let's do it!"

Cow Girl smacked her cheeks and gave a little yell to work herself up. She opened the door of the shed with some force.

She went in, coughing a little at the dust she had stirred up.

The empty room yawned around her. It was one thing to stay here for a night, but who would sleep in such a place all the time?

"Honestly, I can't believe this guy!" Cow Girl put her hands on her hips and made a sound of exasperation.

There was almost nothing in there in the way of personal possessions; all he had was his own body. She wondered what he did about changes of clothing. Something arbitrary, no doubt.

If he thinks I'm going to let him get away with that sort of thing forever...

She started by covering her mouth with a cloth, then took her broom and swept all the trash outside. The shed itself actually seemed in decent shape; perhaps he had been doing repairs.

"Gah! He's *always* been so...so...!"

The improved state of the structure made her a little more reckless with the broom; she could sweep enthusiastically without fear of the place falling down.

Swinging that broom around reminded her of him.

It seemed like they had always been together when they were small. There had been other children their age in the village; maybe it was just because they lived next door to each other.

He loved to run through the fields, swinging a stick around, pretending to be an adventurer. But he didn't know what was beyond the mountains or even what the city was like.

That's why we had that last fight.

Once all the trash was taken care of, she started cleaning the floor.

"I should bring at least a hand towel for him..."

Or maybe just yell at him to sleep in his own room already.

"Yeah, that's it. Yeah. I'll ask him what's wrong with the bed I set up for him."

She could practically picture his older sister with her hands on her hips, scolding him.

I guess it wouldn't be fair to bring her into this.

So she would leave that part out. Just that.

"Phew..."

After she had given the floor a good scrubbing, she squeezed her rag into her bucket of water, immediately turning it black. It was filthy. Maybe that was what they got for leaving this place alone for so long.

She regarded the room silently. It wouldn't be so easy, she knew. *People's hearts can seem complicated and simple at the same time...but they're definitely complicated.*

She couldn't shake the sense that even this cleaning might all be for nothing.

She hated the way such dark thoughts bounced around in her head.

"Forget it, just work!" she told herself. "Maybe a nice, clean room will change how he feels." She set to scrubbing once more.

Something dribbled onto the floor. Was it sweat or tears? Even Cow Girl herself didn't know.

§

O Goddess, Earth Mother
The god who sows the wind claims
Your chest is worth a thousand pieces of gold
Though one spends money like water,
Whatever comes of it is up to you
Us, we have no money, but
Goddess, O Goddess, come out
Come out to the golden sea

The peasants sang lustily as they worked to collect the crops. Sickles swung, cutting down grain; cabbages were plucked up and radishes pulled from the earth; beans were piled in baskets.

Harvest was always an urgent business, but there was evident enjoyment on the faces of the people. Seeds were planted in autumn, lay dormant through the winter, and now could finally be collected as food. Perhaps the joy was understandable.

The farmers had taken such pains to grow these crops, preparing the soil, keeping a close eye on the sun and wind and rain. Some of the harvest would be converted into money to pay their taxes, but there would no doubt be a good deal left over.

Far be it from them to let some sniveling goblins simply walk in and steal the stuff.

You've come, you've come, Earth Mother
The god who sows the wind claims
Your bottom is like the four directions
Though one spends money like water,
If they have not your love, Goddess, you will not come.
Us, we have no money, but
This, O Goddess, is your wedding procession
We lead you to the golden sea.

The warm sunlight, the breeze in the grass, the song drifting to the ear.

The gentle babble of the irrigation channels, where the water level was gradually rising; the regular creak of the waterwheel.

The sounds, sounds that could be heard only in a farming village like this one, communicated an almost otherworldly idyll.

If one were to sit on the paths between the rice fields to listen, it would be all too easy to pass the time in listening until drifting off to sleep.

He suddenly realized he had been standing there motionless, and he quickly started working his knife again.

There was no time; certainly, there was none to waste in napping.

"..."

First, make the spikes.

That had been his declaration, and in his hands was a stake of plain wood, along with a carving knife. The stake was long enough that it could almost pass for a spear, but it was a simple thing that had been shaved down to a point at both ends.

He brushed the wood shavings off his crossed legs and put the finished stake in a pile beside him.

"Hey, why'd you sharpen both ends of those things?"

Beneath his helmet, he frowned slightly at the interruption.

He glanced over and saw the little girl who had introduced herself to him when he had arrived at the village. The last time he had seen her, she had been weeping copiously from the abbess's scolding, but now, she was all smiles again.

He considered for a moment, then tilted his helmet with its one horn curiously.

"Do you not need to help the others?"

"I don't think they need my help." Oddly, the child puffed out her chest as she spoke with something very near to pride.

"Is that so?"

He all but ignored her and picked up the next stick. *Scritch, scritch.* The entire time his knife worked, the girl stared at him intently.

"......"

"......"

"......"

"......"

After a while, he let out a sigh and said, "They are for posting in the irrigation canals."

"Lots of 'em?"

"Enough to make our enemies think twice about trying to cross them."

The reason they were longish and pointed on both ends was so that they could be stuck in the canals.

His survey of the geography along the border of the village had suggested that where a fence could not be built—in other words, along the fields—the only choice would be to take advantage of the canals.

"More importantly," he said, glancing away from the girl, who was regarding him with some admiration, "the abbess is looking for you."

"Oh, crud!"

Almost before the words were out of his mouth, the girl sped off like a hare. He tried to follow her with his eyes, but she was nothing more than a bit of fluttering black hair at the corner of his vision. She was quite quick. The abbess arrived at a jog, out of breath, but she seemed to have little hope of catching the girl.

"Oh, for goodness'— Pardon her. I did tell her not to bother you."

"Don't worry," he said, shaking his head. "I was not bothered."

He placed the next pared-down stake beside him and again brushed the shavings from his knees. He worked mechanically, dutifully; he seemed to have a sense that he should simply remain nonchalant.

Start by doing what's right in front of you. There isn't and never will be time to worry about the future.

The old rhea had shouted something else at him, too, though: *but never stop thinking!*

Looking back on it, it occurred to him that such contradictory proclamations might simply have been his master saying whatever came to mind at a given moment.

"There may be goblin patrols. They will be less likely to notice anything if all continues as usual."

Still, he continued to let his mind work at the same time as his hands, just as he'd been told.

"Do you really think so?" the abbess responded.

"It's likely," he said, and his helmet shook.

He indicated something just on the edge of the village: a largish stone building, like a funerary structure.

"Is that the warehouse where you store the crops?"

"Yes. And although it's made of stone, it's not an especially sturdy building..." The abbess confessed how embarrassed she was by the fact.

He ignored her, muttering to himself.

In that case, that's the one place the goblins absolutely must not be allowed to enter.

And on the other side of the coin, it's the place the goblins would be most keen on getting into.

"Can I ask you to handle the cleanup of the fence and stakes when the quest is over?"

"I'm sure we don't mind, sir..."

He gathered up the finished stakes, then stood slowly.

"I may not be able to help you."

§

"Okay, everyone, we're now offering a quest to slay the Rock Eater!" Guild Girl shouted at the top of her lungs to make herself heard over the din of the building.

"We're on it!"

"My party'll go!"

"Sure thing!" Guild Girl said as adventurers raised their hands. She rushed to prepare the paperwork.

She was slowly starting to get used to her regular work, but this was the first time she had dealt with a case in which several parties formed an alliance and worked together. Having been entrusted with such a large project, she was set on doing her very best, but…

If I mess up because I don't know what I'm doing, it could turn into a disaster…!

"Er, okay then, please sign this paper, and when you're done—"

"I thought the next thing was—you know. That waiver that says the Guild won't be responsible for any disputes between parties."

"Oh, right! Yes. Pardon me!"

Nervousness had all but robbed her of the ability to think; it was all she could do to listen to the adventurer she was ostensibly helping. She was starting to doubt whether she should be doing work that would affect so many people…

Well, I guess it's a little late for that.

Ever since one of the Dark Gods had been struck down five years before, monsters had been flooding into the world.

The story was that this particular incident had begun with some mining. The miners, searching for a deeper vein, had instead come across lumps of viscous black liquid.

They were a type of Slime, known as Blobs, and they multiplied almost instantaneously, chasing the miners from the mine.

That much was common enough and, indeed, would have been a job that adventurers would have been happy to take.

But that wasn't the whole story this time.

A Rock Eater had appeared from underground.

Although frequently confused with giant centipedes, Rock Eaters were a breed apart from simple bugs. The two were sometimes confused because Rock Eaters had an appearance somewhat like a many-legged insect, but that would be like making no distinction between lizards and dragons.

They were massive creatures that literally consumed rocks, eating their way deep into the earth underneath mountains. Caves, holes, and caverns everywhere in the world were the legacy of hungry Rock Eaters…

Or anyway, so went the myth, although the philosophers of the capital denied it vehemently.

Rock Eaters' penchant for gems meant they were the sign of an especially rich mine—but only so long as they didn't get so close to the surface that they chased Blobs out.

These slow-moving lumps made good prey for a creature that ate rocks; a Rock Eater wasn't going to *dissolve that easily.* And Blobs just had thin carapaces enclosing the rich liquid inside…

It's almost too much.

Just for a moment, when the steady flow of adventurers had briefly abated, Guild Girl put her head on the desk. She turned, laying her cheek on the wood. It felt nice.

"Blob slaying. Sure, they took the job, but…"

If someone were to die—if a party were to get wiped—on a quest I did the paperwork for…

And this was a particularly sudden case. Insofar as Guild Girl hadn't participated in any investigation of the incident prior to assignment, she shouldn't bear any responsibility. But still…

"Ugggggh…"

"Gosh, just when I thought you were getting used to it, there you go being depressed again." *Hang in there.*

The encouragement from her colleague elicited a "Right" and a small nod from Guild Girl. "But doesn't it ever get to you? I mean, wondering whether they'll be all right?"

"Sure, it bothers me, but my worrying won't make things any better, will it?"

"I guess not."

She sat up and picked up her pen with what she hoped was extra gusto, but she just couldn't bring herself to face more paperwork.

When her coworker saw Guild Girl mindlessly spinning the pen in her hand, a knowing smile crossed her face.

"What? Got an adventurer who's on your mind?"

"No, I don't!" Guild Girl said with a pouty look, but her colleague's catlike smile didn't waver.

"Well, tell me about them sometime. Ha-ha. So that's what's been going on…"

"I'm telling you, it certainly isn't!"

"It's bad policy to get too emotionally invested in your adventurers. You have to focus on your work." Guild Girl's colleague gave her an encouraging pat on the shoulder, then went back to her own desk looking perfectly happy.

I mean, sure, but…

Guild Girl repeated the injunction to herself silently, then quickly made sure she was presentable.

Yes, work was work. If she was going to be dealing with adventurers, she had to make sure she looked her best, and—

"Miss Receptionist."

"Eep! Uh, y-yes! Yes?"

The sudden summons almost sent her jumping out of her seat.

The first thing she registered was the odor of alcohol. She frowned—the smell of wine on an adventurer was not one she had good memories of—and then she blinked. A man with a face like a bear was standing in front of her; his clothes were somewhat disheveled, and his beard was unkempt, but his glance was keen.

It was the young warrior who had lost his friend in the first encounter with the Rock Eater some days earlier.

"I'm going, too," he said in a remarkably calm tone. "I'm going. Please, send me, Miss Receptionist."

"Er, um…"

Guild Girl's eyes flitted around the building. There were so many things she ought to say to him, but she couldn't figure out which one to say first. Perhaps it would be best, then, to simply say nothing. Accede to his request. And yet, that felt deeply wrong to her.

Taking on a quest was a voluntary act, and those who accepted a quest were responsible for their own fates. As long as they were of roughly the right rank, that was all there was to it.

This young man was still Porcelain-ranked, as she recalled, but the Rock Eater quest was open to participants of any rank. A Rock Eater that had installed itself in a cave was a fearsome foe but still a far cry from a Dark God or a dragon.

But this adventurer was solo at the moment. He had no party.

"...Are you sure you'll be all right?"

"I'm sure."

"..."

Guild Girl didn't speak for a moment, but she thought of *him*.

Was he fighting goblins by himself right then? Why was it all right for him to go alone but not this young man? Truth be told, she didn't want *him* to go by himself, either, but—

"Perfect, you listened." A raucous voice cut through her reverie. She looked up to see a giant of a warrior with a broadsword across his back. "Consider him temporarily part of my party, then."

"..."

Guild Girl didn't say anything right away. The young warrior chewed his lip and then said simply, "Thanks."

Heavy Warrior shrugged without a word. Behind him, his party members exchanged wry looks.

"Miss Receptionist."

This time, Guild Girl let out a soft breath.

Adventurers took responsibility for themselves. Maybe that was enough. She could only give her utmost to the work she had to do.

"Very well. Good luck," she said and then bowed deeply.

§

For now, strengthening the fence is most important.

The sun was slowly sinking, turning the sky dark crimson. *He* continued his work silently.

The last light of day flung itself into his room at the temple, bathing the plain stone chamber in a dazzling array of colors. The play of light from the westering sun over the cheap-looking helmet made it look even more uncanny than usual. The girl and the other children had come to peek into his room, but when they saw him, they had given little squeals and ran away with no sign of coming back.

"..."

In the otherwise empty temple room, he selected wood from the pile beside him and arranged it into groups. He had several large, round sticks freshly cut from the mountain to the north. He crossed them one over another and looked at them—maybe they could make a fence.

"Hmm......"

He thought back to his encounters with goblins to date. How large had they been? No bigger than children. *Except the hobs.*

In that case, the question became how to space the vertical and horizontal members of the fence. Most people thought a sturdy fence was enough by itself to keep out enemies, but one had to consider the possibility of the foe climbing it. If the horizontal members ran too close, they would be easy to scale.

And yet, as the goblins' nickname, "little devils," suggested, they were physically small. If the crosswise bars were too far apart, they would simply sneak through.

"In that case..."

The obvious thing was to space the vertical members closely.

He put together the wood, tying it down tight to make the fence. Then he let out a breath. His jury-rigged barrier looked almost like a ladder lying on its side, but it would serve for defense. It would be difficult for goblins to get through or over.

Suddenly, a thought crossed his mind: *I'll have to make one for the farm at some point.*

He slowly shook his head, blinking beneath his helmet. Another gentle shake made him realize his temples were throbbing. When he thought about it, he recalled that he had been on the move ever since morning.

He pulled a waterskin from his luggage and took two long swigs. Then he brought out a piece of dried meat, slicing it into thin strips with his knife, which he then inserted through the visor of his helmet.

Each time he chewed, his barely moist mouth was filled with an unpleasant saltiness.

He leaned back against the wall and closed his eyes, focusing entirely on the act of chewing the meat. His tongue hurt something awful. Perhaps it was the salt? He took another pull from his canteen, swallowing the drink and the meat in one gulp.

He stood slowly. Once he refilled his waterskin, he would most likely have to stay on watch for the night.

The goblins would almost certainly send scouts.

He left the temple. Outside, the last rays of twilight shooting over the horizon seemed piercingly bright. He held up his hand against the light and looked at the sky. When twilight was clear, his sister had told him, there would be fair weather the next day. If the last light of day was a dark red, however, it meant there would soon be rain.

"So it's rain."

The decisive battle would take place the next night. It would be best if it didn't rain. At the very least, not in the morning.

But perhaps rain would come. If it did, what then? He was not optimistic about the outcome.

How would the goblins attack? That was the question he entertained as he walked along. Finally, he arrived at the now high-running irrigation channels, where the farmers, finished harvesting, were just washing their hands.

He greeted everyone briefly, then began to fill his canteen.

"How's the harvest?"

"Fair enough, I guess," said the farmer who had gone to get him wood that morning. He had a face baked dark by the sun; now he wiped it with a cloth he had dipped in the canal. He smiled gently. "Better than it was five years ago, with the war 'n' all. Them monsters came and trampled our fields, burned our villages…"

"Yes," he said with a nod. "I know."

"I suppose you would, sir, bein' an adventurer and all."

"…"

The man chuckled merrily, then plopped himself down beside the canal. He was looking not at the adventurer who stood beside him but at the sun nearly sunk below the horizon.

"Back then...only the villages us adventurers went to survived."

He was silent, watching the red light stretch out over the land. However desperately the light might cling to the soil, when night came, it would slip away, and the board would be cast into darkness. Then, it was the goblins' time. How gladly they would move across it.

"I will do what I can," he said finally, and then he started walking slowly toward the fields.

That night, he saw hazy illumination, like ghost lights, flickering out beyond the fields.

Stationed near the storehouse, he rose to his feet several times, believing that a goblin attack had come.

It turned out, however, that the lights were nothing more than lamps the villagers used on patrol.

But still, he couldn't shake the feeling that they were the burning eyes of goblins.

Was he fighting goblins now, or wasn't he? As he passed the night with one eye shut and one open, his sense of reality became muddied, ambiguous.

He stood, looked around, sat down silently, and then stood again. Once each hour he would do this, waiting on tenterhooks.

What was he waiting for—goblins or the dawn? He himself didn't even know.

It was dawn that came first.

§

Even a cursory count of the adventurers gathered at the entrance to the mines indicated forty or fifty people, suggesting well over ten different parties were participating. As alliances went, it was only average size, and the highest-ranking adventurers could be forgiven if they breathed a sigh.

A Copper-ranked adventurer, a man in shining armor, vigorously waved a war fan to command attention. "All right, listen up! Our enemy is at the bottom of the mine! So we're going to take the miners' paths and surround him on every side!"

The man's neatly trimmed beard and the sword at his hip gave him a distinguished air and made him look like one of those nobles who sometimes played at being an adventurer. But one could not achieve a high rank by landholdings and reputation alone.

"This guy looks like he's more fit for city living than underground combat," muttered Spearman, who had been assigned to a party of Porcelains at the vanguard.

Still, at least they had a Copper rank to lead them. From what Spearman had seen, the man was actually a fairly capable fighter. A quick look around revealed that most of the people there were Porcelain or Obsidian, barely more than beginners.

Of course, Spearman was hardly in a position to judge, but he had made it through a fight or two at least. Any newbies who had chosen this for their first job because it sounded cooler than goblin slaying, though...

"This is monster killing, right? Couldn't they at least have brought a couple barrels of oil? There're Blobs down there."

"Dumbass," a voice said, putting a hand on Spearman's shoulder. "Take this many people in a space that confined and add fire? Total wipe, I guarantee it." The speaker was a heavy warrior with a broadsword across his back. "And the quest giver is the owner of the mine. I don't think he'd be happy if we blew up his property."

"And what? You think all these people are just going to go along quietly?"

"This isn't some small-scale expedition. Take a good look around. Somebody here might end up saving your neck."

"You can always tell who the party leaders are. They sure know how to talk."

Don't push it, Heavy Warrior advised, frowning, and then went back to his companions.

In his group, a half-elf fighter was keeping an eye on two youngsters.

"Okay, now, do just like we did with those goblins, and you'll be fine," the half-elf said.

"Y-yeah. Obviously...," the scout boy said.

"Conserve your spells. Blobs are one thing, but Rock Eaters are serious opponents."

"Yessir," the druid girl answered. Both kids nodded seriously. They glanced in Heavy Warrior's direction, and he gave them an encouraging smile. It would give them some relief to know that their *leader* was looking out for everyone.

"How about you?" Heavy Warrior called out. "Looking good?" He was talking to a female knight, who was getting her gauntlet on with a somewhat tense expression. They fit securely over her hands, like gloves.

The knight looked over at the warrior, flicking back her long, golden hair. "I'm fine," she said, the strain clear on her face. "More importantly, where's my helmet?"

"Good point, we'll want to be wearing those. Hey, helmets! Headgear!"

"On it!" Scout Boy rifled through his belongings and pulled out what amounted to a headband, while Half-Elf Fighter nodded and put on a leather cap. Druid Girl adjusted her headwear, something like a broad-brimmed hat.

In the midst of all this, Heavy Warrior came around behind Female Knight, looking exasperated. "Why would you put on your gauntlets *before* your helmet? Some things never change..."

"O-oh, be quiet. I lost track a little bit. Simple mistake."

"It stops being a mistake when it happens every time." He took a breath. "Forget about it. Just hold still."

Female Knight grunted in annoyance but didn't move. Heavy Warrior bundled up her golden hair with a somewhat unpracticed hand, holding it in place with a hair clip behind her head.

"Why let it get so long? It just gets in the way."

"Well, pardon me for wanting a touch of womanliness."

"*Is that it?*" Heavy Warrior muttered, taking a helmet from his bag. Female Knight accepted it with a small measure of panic and did the fasteners with more than a little complaining.

Heavy Warrior also produced a new leather helmet for himself, putting it on and tying the chinstrap. Now they were ready.

"What about you?" he asked. "Ready to go?"

"Yeah."

He was speaking to the young newbie warrior.

Well, "young"—he wasn't so different in age from Heavy Warrior, neither of them more than fifteen or sixteen years old. He was different from Scout Boy and Druid Girl, who had had to lie about their ages, so Heavy Warrior was less worried about him. If anything, he looked quite competent as he checked over the condition of his armor and weapons.

"Looks like this isn't your first adventure."

"I went goblin slaying, once."

"Goblin slaying?" Heavy Warrior murmured, frowning openly. The memory embarrassed him.

"Don't press him," interjected Female Knight, who had overheard the conversation.

"What's all that about?" asked Spearman, and Female Knight eagerly told him the story of her leader's failure. Although her helmet hid her expression, there was no doubt that she was smirking behind her visor.

"I don't see that one kinda weird guy," Heavy Warrior said, pointedly changing the subject.

"Who?"

"The one who's always talking about goblins."

"Oh, him," the young warrior said, taking his own helmet in hand. Then he added with absolute dispassion, "I'm sure he's off slaying goblins somewhere."

§

From the village came merry voices, mixed with the sound of music and the aroma of a burning fire.

The source you know, but whither does it go? Its true form you guessed, yet it's not manifest. An old riddle his teacher had posed to him.

He picked up his things and started walking away, seeking some distance from the commotion. His only companions as he went were the fading sounds and smells of the festival.

The first light of summer seemed hot enough to burn, his bag bit into his shoulders, and every step seemed heavy.

But a step was a step.

Put one foot out, move your body forward, then the next foot, body forward.

One step.

If you took one step over and over, you would move forward. The steps would pile up, until eventually, you got where you were going.

Time, and strength of body, were limiting factors, but still, there was no place one couldn't reach with enough walking.

So he gritted his teeth and walked, and when he had reached the outskirts of the village, he discovered a place for himself.

"..."

First, let down the luggage. He was carrying the defensive fence he had made the day before, and of course, his intention was to set it up. Given how short goblins were, it wasn't necessary for the fence to be very high, but it still weighed a fair amount.

Pikes in the river, and where there was no river, a fence. There was no time to be enjoying himself at some festival.

But as for the villagers, I need them to enjoy their little party.

If all the villagers suddenly turned out to work on the defenses, the goblins would be sure to notice. They might go to work on that information with their nasty little brains, and it would end up making things worse.

"Hrm..."

Thus, he summoned all his strength and set to work. Quietly, sweat streaming down his brow, he anchored the fence in the earth, secured it with rope, and then moved on to the next piece.

When he ran out of fence, he had to go back to get more, and when he came to the river, he went to get the stakes, and then he continued with his work. He liked this sort of thing: working intently, mechanically, not thinking anything.

He wasn't all that good at thinking, anyway. His older sister and his master had not been shy in telling him this.

In truth, he fully recognized that he was, perhaps, a little stupid.

So keep thinking!

His master had bellowed those words at him, and he had no desire to turn his back on his teacher's instructions, but thinking was such tiring work. Sometimes it was a relief to be able to simply focus on what was in front of him. He liked that most of all.

Right now, all he had to think about was erecting the fence and getting the stakes in the river.

Goblins.

Yes, this was in order to protect the village from goblins.

Goblins. Goblins...

With each piece of fence he put up, he thought about killing one goblin. He thought about the same thing with each pike he sank in the river.

It was like a daydream: cut with his sword, or smash with his shield; slice the throat, sever the spine.

How would he kill them? What process would he use? In what way would he attack; how would he stop their breathing?

He had learned as much as it was possible to learn from his previous battles.

Goblins were weak. One on one, they were hardly a threat. A villager could chase one off with a stick, even kill it.

The question was how to do that many, many times in a row.

Enter the cave. Were there ten enemies? Twenty?

In the worst case, he might have to cut down twenty foes with his sword. He would need stamina.

And his weapon: a master with the blade could focus every strike, but he was swinging practically at random. The edge of his sword might chip against bone, or become dull with fat as it cut through flesh.

And what do I do then?

His hand stopped moving, and he stared at the sky. There was no answer there. No one to tell him what to do.

Use a club? No—it was easy enough to swing, but swinging was about all it could do. From the perspective of versatility...

"No."

That wasn't it. He slowly shook his head.

He could hear the festival in the distance. He suddenly had the sense that a familiar voice had called his name.

Score one, and it's a beer for an adult, a lemonade for a child.

He had practiced often.

He was good at throwing things. He'd always been ready to boast about how he did this for the sake of his older sister, and the neighbor girl.

"The fence," he muttered. "Must build the fence."

He reached for his cargo, only to find that he had already used up all the fence he had brought with him.

And that wasn't all: he discovered he had already circled the village. The piece of fence he had just put up stood next to another piece; all he had to do was tie them together.

On the other side of the fence was open field, and the north mountain in the distance. The villagers said it was a mine.

He gave the untied fence an offhanded kick. It groaned under the impact and wobbled, creating a little gap.

"..."

He took a close look at it, then gazed up once more at the sky. It was obvious how the goblins would interpret this.

The sun was nearly gone. Twilight was all over the western sky, and he could all but hear the cry of the thunder dragon.

Here, he finally realized that he had eaten nothing since that morning. He poured more water down his prickling throat. Then he took out some dried meat and forced it into his mouth. Chew, swallow. His throat still seemed dry enough to crack despite the drink of water, but all this was at least enough to help him focus his attention.

He crouched among the bushes and took out a torch. It was made of pine resin and sulfur, walnut shells, and dried-out rat and cow dung that had then been treated with alcohol.

He held the torch, waiting for the sun to disappear completely.

And then...

CHAPTER 7

Climax Phase

Night Comes

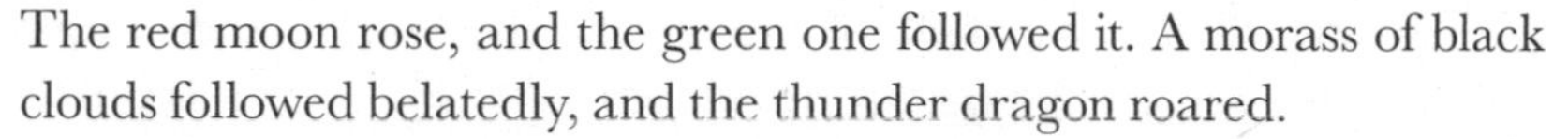

The red moon rose, and the green one followed it. A morass of black clouds followed belatedly, and the thunder dragon roared.

A blue-white light rent the air with something like a bellow, and the first drops of rain began to fall upon the ground.

For the goblins, this was all a blessing from the heavens. A gift from Chaos.

"GORRB! GOBROGBG!"

"GOORBGRGO!"

Although goblins normally cursed rain, it was their way to be glad about anything that suited their needs. The little devils, who had been crouched among the bushes, waiting for their moment, now emerged with vicious smiles on their faces.

Their numbers were many, and they held a variety of crude weapons in their hands, but on every face was the same expression of overweening greed.

They understood the customs of humankind, although there was no telling how they had learned them. They knew that humans sang foolish songs as they harvested their crops, and that after that, they stored everything in a single place. And after putting the crops away, the humans would dance like fools, enjoying themselves.

How stupid humans were, thought the goblins. What was so interesting about all that? They were so easily amused.

The sight of these happy, satisfied humans raised the goblins' ire. Here the monsters were, living in the wilderness, lashed by rain and starving for food, and yet those humans were living in perfect comfort with hardly any effort on their part.

Goblins, by and large, had one way of getting things: they stole them. Thus, no goblin had ever experienced the labor of raising even a single animal as livestock or a single plant as a crop. As far as they were concerned, all these things simply appeared spontaneously, *poof*.

And because the things were there, the goblins thought, they naturally belonged to the goblins. If anything, it was blatantly unfair that the humans should keep all those things for themselves.

The situation was just the same this night.

"GROB! GORB!"

"GOROBG!!"

The goblins' jealousy burned. The humans had chased them away, and that justified all that the goblins would do.

Ever loyal to their basest desires, the goblins poured out and headed for the village.

Food was there. Pleasures. Women.

It would be the perfect way to pass the time before they had to find somewhere to bed down for the night.

These goblins had been chased out of their homes. They had spent several days wandering, and although nothing much had happened, to the goblins, it was nearly unbearable. Resentment ran through them like a current. At that moment, they didn't fear even adventurers.

"GOROBOG?!"

They found their way blocked by a fence. It was no more elegant than a ladder lain on its side, and it hadn't been there yesterday.

The goblin who had been on patrol tried eagerly to explain this away, but it was obvious that the idiot had either overlooked it or simply neglected his duty. Whichever it was, the other goblins surrounded him and beat him with their clubs until he stopped moving.

This was customary for goblins, although none of them believed that they would meet the same fate if they themselves should one day fail.

"GORBG! GOOBOGOR!!"

They attempted to climb the fence, but the crossbeams were spaced too far apart, and they couldn't reach from one to the next. Finally, with much muttering and complaining, the goblins began walking around the fence.

One of them noticed that there was no fence in the river and jumped in, only to find himself impaled on a stake, so the others gave up the notion of fording the stream. They settled for laughing at the moron who had gotten himself skewered; no thought of gratitude to him entered their minds. If anything, they only imagined stabbing the humans who attacked them in just the same way.

Finally, the enraged monsters had made nearly a full circuit of the village. They were on the verge of attempting to break the fence down when they suddenly stopped.

"GOROGORB..."

They had found just one place where the fence was not tied securely.

The goblins looked at one another, smirking. This just went to prove how stupid humans were.

There was no need to break down the fence, deliberately announcing themselves. They would sneak into the village, attack the surprised humans, trample them down.

They pushed their way past the fence, which creaked like an ill-oiled door, and entered the village.

The rain only made them go quicker.

§

He had done what he could do.

He believed he had, anyway.

Really?

He didn't know.

Perhaps there was something else he could have done. Something he forgot.

It would be good if things went well, but—that *if* was questionable.

Everything was his responsibility. The progress, the outcome, were both in his hands.

What, are you gonna run away?

Calm down. Breathe deeply. Calm. Breathe again.

That was all just emotions.

Not reality.

The raindrops beat mercilessly on his body, his breath fogging in the air.

His body was heavy, his fingers stiff as if they were stuck to the hilt of his sword with glue.

I don't know whether I can do it.

He would do it.

That was reality.

If not, he would die.

The reality was exactly that.

If you killed, you would not die.

Reality.

"..."

He lit his torch, rose up from among the reeds, and attacked the nearest goblin.

"GOROG?!"

Before the creature could turn around, he slammed his shield into its back; he drove his sword into the fallen monster's spine and gave it a violent twist.

Start with one.

"GOROOGOROG?!"

"GOBRG! GOORBG!"

The goblins finally registered that their companion had collapsed in the mud and began to turn in his direction.

He threw away his torch. Even in the rain, the flame illuminated the area, the shapes of him and his enemies floating up from the darkness.

A steel helmet with one broken horn, grimy leather armor, a sword of a strange length in his hand, and on his arm, a small, round shield.

How many goblins are there?

Ten, maybe twenty. Certainly not thirty. Five that he could see right at that moment.

They had come through the fence in a row. This was his opportunity to kill them.

"GOROG!!"

"Hmph."

He leaped.

He intercepted the goblin's club against the shield on his left arm, slicing with his sword from hip level. He felt it bury itself in the creature's throat; he gave the sword a twist and then kicked the monster off the end of it.

"GOBORGOGB?!"

"That's two."

"GOBORG!"

A goblin jumped at him from the left, wielding a dagger; he blocked it with his shield. The blade bit into the leather with a thump. He left it there, using his now-free sword to cut a diagonal slash through a goblin to his right.

"GORRROBGOGORG?!"

"Three. No…"

The cut was too shallow. He clucked his tongue. He immediately twisted his body, driving his sword into the gut of the goblin trying to extract its dagger from his shield.

"GOGGROGB?!"

The creature gave an inarticulate scream and fell to the ground, trying to hold back its overflowing innards.

It was alive. But the wound was fatal. He could afford to leave that one to die.

"Three, and this makes four…!"

"GORORG?!"

He turned to the goblin to his right, which was wobbling back and forth and bleeding from its chest. He brought his sword down from overhead.

There was a *thock* as the sword sank into the monster's brain; it tumbled backward, its brains splattering everywhere. He gave the body a hurried kick to free his weapon, lest the sword be pulled away from him by the falling corpse.

The blade was chipped now. He clucked his tongue again. The rain was terribly cold, an ache creaking through his body.

"Next…!"

The village was enclosed on all four sides, and he had left them a tiny hole to find. He had known they would come after the festival. He had been sure they would push their way in through the gap.

It had only been a matter of waiting for them.

"GORRRG!"

"GROBRG! GGORG!"

He saw one set, then two, of ghostly goblin eyes approaching through the dark.

"Goblins…," he said in an eerily calm, quiet voice. If anyone had been around to hear it, they might have mistaken it for a wind blowing from the depths of the earth.

"I'll kill them all."

§

"Something's coming!!"

The Copper-ranked leader's instructions had been nothing if not on the nose: if the Rock Eater had chased the Blobs out of their home, then they simply needed to go in the direction where there were no Blobs.

One of the scouts heard a rumble and stopped, but no sooner had he issued his warning than his head vanished. It was bitten off with a dry sound, like a nut cracking open, by a pair of giant jaws that appeared from the rock face.

"CEEEEENNTI!!"

The monster that had dug its way through the depths of the mine stuck its head out in front of the adventurers, its mandibles gnashing. In front of it, the headless scout twitched once and then fell to his knees. It was only a moment later that the blood spewed out. The other adventurers shifted into fighting stances.

"Y-yikes…"

"It's… It's really here…"

"Well, obviously!"

The first to shout and ready his weapon was Spearman. He forced his way through a troupe of adventurers wearing unblemished armor to take up a position in the front. Even he, who had dreamed of doing deeds of valor in battle with notorious monsters, was stiff-faced now.

It might have been a myth to say this monster dug out mountains by itself, but even so, between its head and its many body segments, the creature must have been more than fifty meters long. They might as well have been facing down a giant.

"And they thought they would send Porcelains on this mission?! —Hey!"

Witch stood level with him. "Ahem! *Sagitta... Quelta... Raedius! Strike home, arrow!*"

Her cheeks glistened with sweat as her luscious lips formed the words of true power. A Magic Missile flew from her staff directly at the Rock Eater, but—

"CEENNTTTTTTTTII!!"

The monster shrugged off the bolt against its shell as easily as a person might brush off a drop of rain.

If it wasn't damaged, though, it was certainly angered. It opened its huge, noisy jaws and flung itself straight at Witch.

"Look out!"

"Eek!"

It turned out to be good fortune that Spearman had taken no action. Now his reaction was instantaneous; he swept Witch up from the side, pulling her out of the way by a hair's breadth.

The Rock Eater slammed into the ground, and then with its countless spindly limbs working, it dug down deeper.

It would have been perfectly fine had the monster simply run away at that point. But the rumble beneath them let them know that this was merely a moment in which to prepare for the next ambush.

"Sorry, about, that..."

"Don't mention it. But we've gotta be careful where we move...!"

Spearman crouched low, covering Witch, who was all but immobilized from shock. There was no telling where that massive head would appear next. If it came from directly below them, there would be no avoiding a critical hit.

"Looks like we aren't going to be keeping this thing down with spells," the heavy warrior with the broadsword on his back said, looking calmly around.

There were about ten adventurers in the narrow mineshaft. All were seized with the terror of not knowing where the next attack would come from.

If we aren't careful, it could wipe us all out at once.

"Spell casters, emphasize support and defense. We'll crush it with physical damage! Anyone in light armor, fall back, and go get in touch with the main group!"

"R-right!"

"Anyone with ranged weapons, though, stay here and—"

"Eccyaaahh!"

Heavy Warrior was interrupted by a woman's scream.

Everyone looked and discovered an archer writhing in pain, her face covered in goo. Every time the black, tar-like stuff moved, steam would rise up, accompanied by the smell of searing flesh.

"Aah—aaggh! Gaaahhgh! Helb mee—helllbb meee!"

The woman clawed at her face and neck, shouting as best she could. She rolled on the ground and struggled. Her party was attempting to dislodge the goo with weapons wrapped in cloth treated with anti-acidic compounds. But her face was being steadily melted away by the Blob.

She's beyond help.

"Blob?!"

"She's in a fight with a Blob!"

Slime-type monsters like these commonly dropped down from above, surprising their prey.

Frowning, Female Knight raised her sword above her head. It shone brightly with Holy Light. It clearly illuminated a wriggling mass of dark stuff on the ceiling, squeezing out of a narrow side tunnel.

"I didn't think there was supposed to be a shaft here...!" she exclaimed.

"Some idiot must've dug it out!" Heavy Warrior shouted.

It was exactly the sort of narrow, dark side route that could easily become home to *goblins or worse*. It would be impossible for any of them to go in there themselves—their only options were to plug the hole or clean it up some other way. But they had no time. If they dawdled, the Rock Eater would consume them all.

Half-Elf Fighter looked queasy. "This might be…the other way around," he said.

"What do you mean by that?"

"I mean, maybe the Blobs weren't chased out by the Rock Eater." He looked around as he spoke, never letting his vigilance falter. "We tried to mine in the Rock Eater's hole. Then the Blobs come here looking for food…"

"They're symbiotes…!" Druid Girl said, her face drawn. "So we're prey to them?!"

"Bah! We can worry about the academic stuff later!" Female Knight shouted, brandishing her cross-sword, the sign of her faith. "Right now, we have to kill them before we get eaten!"

"You think you're ever gonna make paladin with that attitude, muscle-brain?" Heavy Warrior used the flat of his broadsword to crush one of the Blobs, then looked at his companions. "We can't count on linking up with the main group now. Give me an enchantment!"

"S-sure!" Druid Girl said. She began to pray, her face tense.

"I need you on this, too!"

"Yes, of, course…" Witch, bracing herself with her staff, began to weave a spell.

An instant later, Heavy Warrior's broadsword began to glow red, and the light of magic shone from the tip of Spearman's weapon.

"O my god of judgment, let not my sword judge that which is good!"

Female Knight intoned a request for a miracle to the Supreme God, casting Blessing upon her own weapon.

There was a terrible rumble; the Blobs vibrated, and dirt rained down on them from overhead.

"The rest of you, deal with these Blobs! Don't let them get near us!"

"Got it! You can count on us!"

In response to Heavy Warrior's order, the other adventurers quickly formed a perimeter.

©Shingo Adachi

You can come out any time now. I'm gonna kill you...!

The young warrior stood alone, his sword at the ready, his spirit utterly settled.

And so he thrust his sword upward almost before it was possible to detect the alarming vibration from overhead.

"Th-there it is!"

The ceiling broke open. Rocks came falling down, followed by a pair of massive jaws. The jaws that had swallowed *her.*

Her body is still inside that thing!

The thought was like an explosion of light in the warrior's mind. He paid no heed to the fact that the monster's fangs were biting into his own arm as he drove the sword upward with both hands, perfectly happy with this stalemate.

He forced the blade up and up, burying it up to the hilt in the insect's throat, warm fluids from the Rock Eater's body pouring over his head.

And then, with the abruptness of a snapping thread, the warrior's consciousness gave way to darkness.

§

As *he* fell, he realized that the momentary loss of consciousness was because he had taken a stone to the head.

He tumbled face-first into a muddy puddle, the rainwater working its way through the slats of his visor, threatening to drown him.

Weak though goblins were, if he hadn't been wearing a helmet, he might have been in real danger.

He put his arms out and began to push himself up, only to feel a severe impact against his back, robbing him of his breath: a blow from a club.

Almost before he could process what had happened, another hit came, and another, and another, and another. There must have been an ax or something among the weapons, because he heard his armor and chain mail shatter, felt the pain of flesh and bone tearing and breaking.

He cursed with the burning agony of it, and the curse tasted like iron in his mouth.

"GOROGR!!"

"GRRB! GOOROGRB!!"

The goblins were laughing. They taunted the stupid adventurer, reveled in bringing him low. No doubt they would soon push on to the village.

And then what would happen?

You mustn't dare move from this spot.

He stuck a hand in the mud. His bones creaked. His knees were bent. His breath was strained. He began to drag himself up.

"GOOBRGBOG!!"

This time the shock of agony ran through his jaw as a club caught him on the side of the face. He rolled over on the ground, landing on his back.

Some of the raindrops fell through his visor and onto his face. His whole body was getting soaking wet, and he was cold. So cold.

Just for a second, he closed his eyes. His sister would scold him for playing in the mud. Then he opened them. He felt his head start to rise; a goblin had grabbed on to the remaining horn on his helmet.

He was dragged to his knees; his vision filled with the goblins' ugly, vulgar grins.

His hand scrabbled, seeking for some way to grab hold of his sword. It had fallen in the mud and, somewhere in the chaos, had been broken. The hilt and pommel were there, but most of the rest of the sword was not. He tossed it aside.

"......"

He said nothing. Mud spattered below him. The goblins cackled, their chattering laughter becoming a buzz inside his helmet.

He saw a club come up; he watched it dimly.

He knew that in just a matter of instants, that club would come down, his helmet would be cracked open, his skull broken, his brains scattered.

They might not manage it in one strike, but two or three would do the job.

He would die.

He felt as if *that* night had pursued him, caught him.

What's the use of your life flashing before your eyes? his teacher had asked.

Think about what you're going to do, right up till your very last moment.

What was he going to do and how?

He silently dropped his eyes.

He knew what had happened to his older sister; he'd watched it happen without making a sound.

He knew what the goblins would do when they got to the village and then that town.

Faces floated through his mind: The neighbor girl. The farm owner. The Guild receptionist. The various adventurers.

What's it to me?

He inhaled deeply, then let his breath out.

It would be the height of arrogance to imagine that the world would fail to go on without him.

Let one village be destroyed; the world would go on. Let one man die; the world would keep turning. The dice would continue to be cast.

And so he would focus only on what was in front of him.

The goblin standing in front of him was holding a club. It was the goblin behind him who was holding the horn on his helmet.

Both his hands were free. Beneath his helmet, he moved his eyes. The goblin in front of him was holding a club.

What about the one behind him, then? He couldn't turn his helmet. Only his eyes.

At the goblin's belt, he noticed, was a dagger.

The hilt was made in the shape of a hawk. He recognized it. It had no sheath.

What's it to me?

His right hand moved like a flash.

"GBOR?!"

He caught a finger in the hawk's beak, pulling the dagger free of the belt; he grabbed it in a reverse grip and brought it down.

That was all.

But when that succeeded in piercing through a goblin's shoulder, severing the spinal column and causing it to die, that was enough.

"GOROBOGOROBOG?!"

The goblin, on the cusp of bringing its club down, instead tumbled backward. Blood boiled from the wound, accompanied by an eerie whistling sound. The blood joined the rain in spattering on him.

The goblin clinging to him from behind was gibbering something.

What's it to me?

He was already tossing aside the dagger, grabbing the club from the newly dead monster.

He swung it as if he were going to strike his own shoulder with it and heard the enemy's arm and shoulder being crushed in.

"GBOGROB?!"

An earsplitting screech. The goblin fell back, clutching its arm. The horn splintered noisily and fell away.

What's it to me?

As he spun, he brought the club down on the goblin's skull. The skin of its head was remarkably soft, caving in slightly as if to accommodate the weapon as it came down to split the head open.

He nonchalantly took a hand ax from the goblin's corpse, which lay there with one eye lying free of its socket. His back ached terribly, perhaps from being struck by this very ax earlier.

What's it to me?

He spun the ax as hard as he could, and then, without hesitation, he released it. It spun through the air, then buried itself in the head of a goblin who had been quite relaxed up to that point.

It was the one who had hit him with the rock earlier. This was easier than winning lemonades, the adventurer thought.

"This makes…ten, and three…!"

He swallowed something stringy and thick in his mouth, yelling out.

He plunged his hand into his item bag and pulled out a bottle. A stamina potion. He popped the cork and swallowed the liquid in a single gulp. It was bitter, and it burned as it flowed down his throat, directly into his stomach.

Immediately, a warmth began to spread through his body. His wounds were not being healed, but his senses were returning. That meant he wasn't dead. So there was no problem.

He threw the bottle away where it sank into the mud; it filled with water and was soon lost to sight.

©Shingo Adachi

"How many left...?

The rain pounded down, and the wind howled. Somewhere through the ink-black night, he could see the ghostly lights of what he assumed was a third division of goblins.

He kicked each of the goblins' corpses with his foot, rolling them over until he found a suitable sword, which he took for himself. He tried to stash it in his scabbard but realized it didn't fit; he would have to carry it in his hand.

What in the world had he been so worried about before? An armory had practically come marching right to him.

"Fourteen...!"

One goblin was trying to squeeze through the fence to get at the village, and he leaped upon the creature.

"GOORBGRB?!"

The monster found a sword through its throat; it frothed and died still hanging on the blade.

He let the body drop away, grabbing a dagger from the creature's belt as it fell and giving it a great swing.

"GOOBG?!"

"Fifteen."

The goblin behind him suddenly found a blade growing from its head; it pitched backward and flailed in the mud.

"GOOROG...!"

"GRORB!!"

Goblins were yowling, but what was it to him? He stepped on the body in front of him, pulling the sword violently from its neck. The blade was drenched with blood, but so what? A substitute would come to him soon enough.

He moved forward, dragging his feet through the mud.

Goblins were cowards. They had no desire to die, much less sacrifice themselves for their comrades.

But at the moment, their enemy was only one person. And thanks to him, each of the surviving goblins found their share of booty increased. If they attacked the village now, each of them would have more women and food than they knew what to do with.

"GOGBRRG!!"

"GORB! GOOBBGR!!"

Ultimately, it seemed, greed won out over fear. The goblins set upon him all together, pushing and shoving one another forward.

"Sixteen… Seventeen!"

One foe jumped at him with dagger in hand, but he struck the monster a blow with his shield, dropping it into the muck. As it writhed, he brought his sword around and cut the throat of the goblin to his right.

Rain and mud splattered everywhere, and blood was overflowing. He took his sword in a reverse grip and sliced up the goblin on the ground, from its head to its neck. *Break the spine.*

"GORBBGR?!"

"Two left…"

He let go of the sword and jumped backward quickly, almost rolling. A club came down and crushed the fresh corpse.

Another goblin had tried to use its companion's demise as a distraction in order to kill him. The monster with the club grumbled angrily.

He sank his hand into the mud, picking up the bottle he had thrown away earlier and flinging it.

"GBBB?!"

There was a scream, presumably from the combined pain of the bottle shattering against the creature's face and the mud getting in its eyes.

The goblin stumbled backward, pressing its hands to its face. He ignored it and instead jumped forward, slamming his shield into a goblin who was holding a spear.

"GBRRGBOG?!"

"One more…!"

In a contest of bodily size and weight, a human had the advantage over a goblin. Especially a human in full armor.

The goblin was down in the mud, and he had it by the neck; he felt it break as he pressed the full weight of his body onto his hands.

He crushed its windpipe as it spasmed and emitted a death rattle, and that was the end of it. He took the spear from its hand and turned to the final goblin, which was just then wiping the mud from its face.

"GOROOROGBGB?!"

"Nine—teen…!"

The spear was nothing more than a rock tied to a sharpened stick, but it was enough to pierce a heart. The goblin died with blood flying everywhere as it clawed at the sky.

He kept a firm hold on the weapon, driving it deeper, then let out a breath.

Breathe in, then out. In, out. In, out. In, then out.

He could taste blood deep in his throat. He wanted nothing more than to lie down right there in the mud. His mind hardly worked, and his eyelids were heavy.

His brain, or some deep part of him, was trying to force logic upon him: *drink an antidote.*

The goblins' bodily fluids, their polluted blades, the rain and the mud: they would all get into his wounds and sicken him. He knew that.

He rose unsteadily, like some sort of ghost, and found the bottle in his item pouch. He had done well not to confuse it with the stamina potion earlier. He would need to come up with some way to tell them apart by feel.

His fingers slipped, making it hard to unstopper the cork, but he managed it and drank down the entire bottle of bitter liquid in a single swallow.

"Ah… Ahh…"

It was over.

It had to be.

Yet, he had no sense of accomplishment; he could hardly believe himself that it was finished.

The rain kept falling. There was no hint that dawn was coming. He was alive, and the goblins were dead.

His torch, which he had modified so as not to go out even in weather like this, continued to puff smoke.

He would not fight goblins on an open field again. They belonged in caves, and so did he.

"………! Hrrgh…"

Suddenly, he felt as if a cold hand were mercilessly squeezing his stomach; he collapsed to his knees. With a wet noise, the guts and the rain and the blood and the mud all splashed up together.

His lungs couldn't seem to take in air. He tore the helmet from his head. He pitched forward, supporting himself with his hands, his mouth open. He couldn't inhale. He couldn't exhale.

Scenes flashed through his mind in an instant. His sister. The burning village. Bodies hanging from ropes. Goblins. The west wind.

Something came up his throat and out of his mouth, burning all the way. He coughed and choked, but what emerged was mostly stomach acid.

After a bout of copious vomiting, he inhaled, then forced himself to take a sip from his waterskin.

He rinsed his mouth and spat, then swallowed another mouthful and wiped his lips.

Then, churning the mud, he finished what was left to do, slowly picking up his helmet and putting it back on. He had the distinct sense that it smelled of blood and sweat and vomit.

He looked around, his helmet much lighter without its other horn.

The carnage was absolute. Piles of goblin corpses stretched from the gap he had left in the fence right up to the edge of the village itself.

One, two, three, four, five, six seven eight nine, ten, eleven, twelve, thirteen fourteen, fifteen sixteen seventeen, eighteen, nineteen…

"Nineteen… Nineteen?"

He cocked his head. He braced himself against the nineteenth corpse and pulled out the spear.

Kicking up mud and water, he proceeded at a bold stride back to the village. The fence, the river, the sound of water… The sound of water…

The goblin who had been attempting somehow to avoid the pikes and ford the river let out a scream and collapsed.

"…Twenty."

That was the last goblin.

But it wasn't over. It never was.

CHAPTER 8

Ending Phase

The Battle Ends

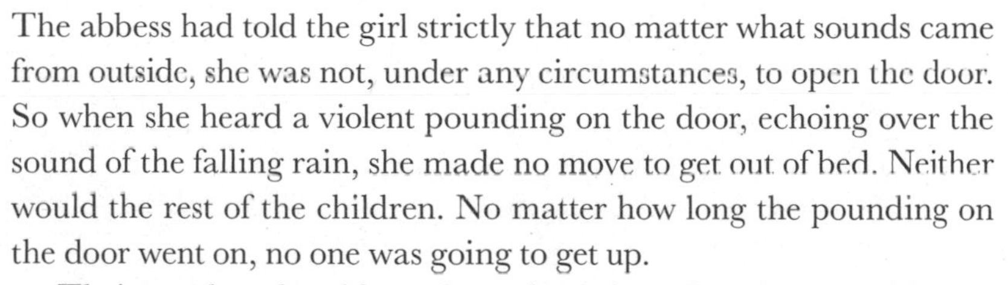

The abbess had told the girl strictly that no matter what sounds came from outside, she was not, under any circumstances, to open the door. So when she heard a violent pounding on the door, echoing over the sound of the falling rain, she made no move to get out of bed. Neither would the rest of the children. No matter how long the pounding on the door went on, no one was going to get up.

Their teacher the abbess showed no sign of getting up, either; it seemed the girl was the only one awake.

But it'd be all right just to see who it is, wouldn't it?

Hence, she slid out of her sleeping spot. All the children had been gathered in the great room together and remained wrapped in their blankets, unmoving.

Cowards, the girl thought as she felt her way along, clutching a broom with both hands. With her improvised weapon firmly in her grasp, she proceeded hesitantly around the nighttime temple.

The candles had been doused early ("lest we waste them"), so it was truly dark. The chapel lay under a veil of silence, the towering image of the Trade God in shadow, looking strangely severe.

Outside, the storm raged—indeed, howled, like a mournful spirit.

The girl was just starting to regret having gotten up, when, as she neared the door, the knocking sound came again.

"Who…? Who is it? Can we…help you…?"

There was a beat, and then a very low voice came from the other side of the wooden portal.

"My work is finished. I've come to report."

Immediately, the girl's face shone, and she ran to the door. She braced herself against the well-oiled bar, and with a "Hmph!" she managed to slide it open.

The abbess had told her not to open the door no matter *what* sound came from outside, but not "no matter *who* came from outside."

So this is fine!

The bar slid neatly free, and the door slowly opened.

Standing there with the storm at his back was a single man. He was cloaked by the darkness, but she saw the unmistakable form of the adventurer she had come to know over the past two days. The cheap-looking helmet, the grimy leather armor, the sword hanging from a scabbard at his hip, and the round shield tied to his arm.

Just one thing was different, perhaps: he was now missing the other horn on his helmet.

He took a single step into the chapel, dripping mud.

"Did you take care of the goblins?!"

"Yes," he said. "I killed them."

The young girl looked a little askance at such blunt language. As he drew near, she detected an odor from him such as she had never smelled before.

Mud and sweat. And something else besides. She scrunched up her nose, but he only said to her, "Do you have any medicinal herbs? Any healing miracles?"

"Uh-uh." The girl shook her head. "Mistress Abbess says she never received any miracles."

But what about other medicine? The girl knew about healing potions only by reputation.

"I see..." He sighed deeply on hearing the girl's answer. He appeared to her as little more than a numinous shape, but he was clearly tired.

He did just come from battle.

So it made good sense. When she exerted herself, she got tired. Even when she was only playing.

"Hey, how about you rest a little? Or do you just wanna go home?"

"Go home?"

The girl had asked the question without really thinking about it, just a common courtesy. But he looked at her with absolute perplexity.

"Home...," he murmured, as if hearing the word for the first time.

Home, home, home. He seemed to be chewing it over, taking it in steadily.

Finally, his helmet moved, slowly but surely.

"Yes," he said, as if he couldn't quite believe it. "I will go home."

"Oh... Okay."

"There's"—and he still sounded disbelieving—"someone waiting for me."

The girl nodded. She had been ready to drag him into the temple if she had to, but...

If he wants to go home, then that's what he should do.

For the girl, this temple was home. It had been five years since she had been separated from her parents; she didn't even remember their faces.

But things must be different for him.

"Well then, um, thank you, okay?"

"No," he said, slowly turning around, his hand on the door, about to go back out into the rain. The girl hadn't been quite sure what words to offer to that image. His head shook, and he spoke, as ever, quietly. "It's all right."

Then the door closed noisily.

"Right," the girl said with a small nod, and then she pitter-pattered through the dark chapel and crawled back into her bed.

That night, she had a strange dream.

It would vanish come morning, hazy, indistinct, and fleeting.

She would completely forget that in the dream, she had held a holy sword in her hand, like a true hero.

§

"Finally up, huh?"

When the young warrior came to, he found himself lying pathetically on a mat spread over a flagstone floor.

He tried to sit up, but his head pounded agonizingly in time with his heart, leaving him unable to move.

He discovered his legs and arms were wrapped in bandages, and to judge by the feel, so was his forehead.

He resigned himself to lying prone on the mat.

"Where am I…?" he asked and found that his throat felt like it might split open. "What became of…?"

"The temple of the Earth Mother."

"The Earth Mother…?"

"You know. The one you see all the time when you're walking around town?"

This thoughtful offer of information came from Heavy Warrior, who was sitting beside him. He was also heavily bandaged, but the expression on his face was lighthearted.

"They were kind enough to turn the worship hall into an impromptu medical center," he said.

The young warrior managed to take a slow look around the chapel. Sunlight streamed through the windows—it must be morning already. The sure footsteps of clerics could be heard among the groaning of injured and exhausted adventurers.

The clerics worked tirelessly in caring for them: bringing water here, giving food there, wiping sweat from those who could not move to do it themselves. No doubt they were also the ones who had tended to the young fighter's wounds. Otherwise, he would never have gotten off so lightly after his encounter with that insect's gigantic jaws.

Standing in the middle of it all, giving instructions, was none other than the Copper-ranked leader. Given the way his now unarmored left arm was hanging at his side, it seemed he had done his share of the fighting. Young Warrior regretted his foolishness for having judged the man by his appearance.

"Anyway, we're all just lucky to be alive. You, me, all of us."

"Right…"

Nearby, Heavy Warrior's party members—the fighter and the scout boy and the druid and all of them—were resting, each of them lost in their own thoughts. For some reason, Female Knight was leaning against Heavy Warrior, asleep. She didn't seem like a light burden…

"Hey… What about that awful bug?"

"Dead," the blunt answer came.

Young Warrior, still lying on his side, clenched his fist.

"I hate to tell you," Heavy Warrior added with a shrug, "but you weren't the one who killed it."

It was rough, after you went out. Then Heavy Warrior told him about the life-and-death struggle that had ensued: The Rock Eater rampaging about with its pierced throat. The hail of stones from above them. The Blobs that kept popping out.

The adventurers had staged a brave offensive against what amounted to a tidal wave of the fluid creatures. If it wasn't going to be possible to rejoin the main group, then they would just have to fight a battle of attrition. They worked their way through the Blobs, striking the Rock Eater whenever the opportunity presented itself.

Before long, the main party came to reinforce them, and the adventurers were able to press their advantage…

"Then that smug spear-wielder put it right through the bug's head, and that was it."

"I see…"

"That's life for you," Heavy Warrior said with a frown, unsure how to take the other fighter's noncommittal response. Perhaps it provoked some bad memories. "Things don't always go the way you want them to." Heavy Warrior glanced at the woman sleeping against his shoulder as he spoke. She was no longer wearing the helmet he had helped her with.

When the young warrior asked what had happened, Heavy Warrior just shook his head and laughed, pointing to her melted metal helmet. "Her face'll heal with time, but that thing wasn't so lucky." He gave Female Knight a rather unsubtle poke in the cheek. Her beautiful face fell into a sour expression, and Heavy Warrior laughed again.

"Well, when a woman gets a burn on her face, it costs her an awful lot…"

From that perspective, the helmet could certainly have been said to have fulfilled its duty.

Come to think of it, she said something about wanting to be a paladin, didn't she?

Although the position of knight was not hereditary, training diligently enough in service could well yield military rewards in due course. Proudly serving the country as both knight and noble was, perhaps, one path to paladinhood.

The fact that she had decided to become an adventurer instead hinted at some deeper reason for her choice.

"All I can do is make the best of it when things don't go my way," Heavy Warrior said. "It's the same for all of us."

"Yeah..."

It was true of Heavy Warrior, and it was certainly true of the young warrior as well.

"One thing's true, though: you were the first to go for it. You did what you could, eh?"

Young Warrior thought about that for a moment, then said simply, "I did," and closed his eyes.

He'd done what he could.

He had led his party as capably as he was able.

The first time they had encountered the creature, he had somehow managed to get them out of there with just one casualty.

His other former party members had all left town, but he was still here, adventuring.

He had jumped into the very jaws of that massive insect, the Rock Eater, and stabbed it as hard as he could.

Yes, he was sure he had done all he could.

So forgive me... But I'm not going to do any more for you.

Apologetic words floated through his mind to that girl, who was now gone.

Then he sank once more into unconsciousness.

§

"I'm sorry—just a second—I'll bring some antipyretic herbs!"

"Right, sure thing!"

The acolyte was a little girl, still barely ten years old. Of course, she didn't have the status of a cleric; it would be something of an exaggeration even to call her an apprentice.

She wore a habit of plain cloth, well patched and ill fitting (perhaps she was still too short). It had been given as payment in kind, and now she rolled up its hem and sleeves as she bustled around the chapel.

They grew medicinal herbs in the temple garden, one of their most important acts of service. She grabbed some of the plants they had recently dried from the shelf where they were kept and came scurrying back. She had to get up on a stepping stool and then stand on her tiptoes to reach them, but she didn't complain.

"Here they are!"

"Thank you. I don't need any more help here, so go somewhere you can be useful."

"Right!"

She gave the herbs to another cleric, one of her seniors, then worked a smile onto her tired face as she went pattering off again.

The senior cleric watched her go with a grin. The scurrying girl, like so many other priests and priestesses, was an orphan. She had been abandoned at the temple five years before, right about the time the war was ending. This year, she would be ten years old. Hardly a grown woman but more than old enough to help with the work of healing.

That wasn't exactly the reason she was here, but—

"Heeey! Got another one for ya!"

She stopped in surprise at the unexpected summons, sweat on her brow. She looked up to see a handsome adventurer with a spear supporting another adventurer in leather armor on his shoulder.

"Er, uh, you mean me, sir?"

"Yeah. Sorry to bother you when you're busy. Just tell me where this guy can sleep."

Even Spearman had no intention of pressing such a young girl. The acolyte nodded and said, "This way," leading them into the chapel.

The place was crowded with injured adventurers, but there were still places to rest, on benches and on the floor. In the worst case, the clerics' quarters could even be made available. There would be no particular problem with that.

"Did, uh, was this person also in the fight with the insect...?"

"No. He was slaying goblins, I'm sure."

"What...?"

"I found him collapsed at the edge of town and brought him here. Damn... He's nothing if not trouble."

With evident annoyance, the spearman helped the adventurer slump down on a blanket that had been laid out on the floor, as the acolyte indicated. On closer inspection, the adventurer clad in grimy armor was covered in dark blood and mud.

She would have to wash and clean him and see to any wounds. Not that she was actually capable of such things yet.

"All right, keep an eye on him for me!"

"Y-yessir!"

Since he had been entrusted to her, there was nothing to be done.

The acolyte nodded vigorously at the spearman several times, then watched him go.

Hey... Didn't they say that it was a spear-wielding adventurer who finished off the monster...?

Could it possibly be him?

Even as her eyes followed him with a questioning look, the girl was already bustling out of the chapel, going to her senior for instructions.

"We don't have enough hands!" the older priestess said. "If his wounds aren't serious, then just leave him for now."

"Hey, where are the fresh bandages?"

"If you change the dressings too often, you'll put them at risk..."

"Just don't reuse them. As long as they're clean, that's enough!"

We'll see to him later. The acolyte stood there dejectedly at this verdict from her overworked seniors.

But there wasn't even time to stand around.

"Here, bandages! Wash these!" someone said, foisting a load of dirty dressings on her. They were covered in crimson smears and stains.

"Oh, r-right!"

The acolyte hurried off with her hands full of laundry, but she managed a glance toward the wall.

There was the adventurer who had been set down earlier, looking exhaustedly at the ground.

Isn't there anything I can do for him?

©Shingo Adachi

What, though? The acolyte didn't know. Maybe she would know someday in the future, when she had much more experience.

It was a very difficult question for a ten-year-old girl.

She scrubbed the bandages in cold water until her hands started to hurt, but still nothing came to her.

The water quickly turned dark and red from the washing, but no matter how many times she got new water, it never seemed to stay clear.

Get fresh water, scrub, get fresh water, scrub, get fresh water, scrub, get fresh water, scrub…

As she worked silently, the acolyte suddenly discovered that there was an empty space inside her. Her hands kept moving, and even her thoughts remained focused. But there was an opening, a void, there in her consciousness, and she seemed to be floating in it.

What's going on? she wondered vacantly, but her heart was strangely calm.

The sound of the water as she washed seemed terribly far away. So did the chill on her skin, and the commotion in the chapel. She perceived all those things but was somehow cut off from them.

Empty.

Although her eyes remained open, in her heart she closed them. And even as her hands worked, in her heart, she clasped her hands together.

She did all this spontaneously, as if it were the most natural possible thing for her.

Protect, heal, save.

The fundamental precepts of the Earth Mother. The most important things.

Suddenly, she connected them to the image of the adventurer languishing against the wall.

O Earth Mother, abounding in mercy, lay your revered hand upon this child's wounds.

At that moment, the acolyte felt as if she herself were enveloped by something, as if she were being pulled bodily upward.

A gentle light glowed in her hand, and she didn't know if it was only in her mind or in reality.

A shimmer bubbled up, and she thought she saw it flying toward *him.*

"Wh-wha...?!"

Almost instantaneously, a tremendous fatigue struck her, and the acolyte let out an involuntary gasp. Her ears were filled with something akin to ringing as the sounds all around her came rushing back.

The acolyte felt as if the ceiling and the ground were trying to switch places; she clung to the washbasin to stave off the dizziness.

The smells of soap and water, and blood, too, all sealed her nose together.

"Haah—ah—haa—wha...? Wh-what was...that...?"

She found she had started sweating profusely; droplets fell from her face into the wash water, *ploop, ploop, ploop.*

A miracle had just occurred, but as yet, there was no one who realized it.

CHAPTER 9
After Session
Between Adventures

"Heeeey, receptionist—I'll take this quest!"

"Certainly!!"

The Adventurers Guild was bustling again today.

Things didn't stop just because one huge monster had been vanquished. There were always more adventures to go on, and more paperwork to do related to those adventures. Bandits making the roads dangerous, evil wizards holed up in various fortresses, vampires in search of influential young women.

Although it was just a rumor, there was even talk that a tribe of centaurs was going to attack.

And then, of course, there was goblin slaying.

Guild Girl, who could no longer be considered new to the job, was scurrying about like a jumping mouse, helping out quest givers, preparing and posting the paperwork for those quests, and working with adventurers who had come to take them on.

Lunchtime finally came, but as soon as she finished eating, it was straight back to work. There was hardly time to relax; she was so busy, her head threatened to spin.

Even so, she had a smile on her face: she had a certain piece of paperwork that she had been working on in every spare moment.

"Oh-ho-ho. What's this?" her colleague asked, taking a peek at the paper, a sandwich still in her mouth. Guild Girl, grinning, laid the paper out for her to see, and she blinked. "An application for promotion in rank?"

"Correct!"

"Oh, I get it—there were an awful lot of Porcelains helping with that Rock Eater, weren't there?"

A number of things went into determining an adventurer's rank: their adventuring résumés, the total amount of rewards they had received, the amount of good they had done the area they lived in, and their personalities, among other things. Clearing out a monster that had taken up residence in a mine would certainly advance anyone's cause for promotion. Assuming there were no glaring flaws in their personality, they could well expect to gain a level immediately.

But then her colleague stopped with a mystified "Hmm? Wait a second… I don't think this guy was even on that adventure, was he?"

"Oh, that's right. He wasn't." Guild Girl shook her head, her braids waggling in time.

Then, however, she showed her colleague *his* adventure sheet with great pride.

"This person is working very hard," she said. "Extremely hard. All by himself."

"Huh. Gosh," her colleague said, chewing her sandwich thoughtfully and looking at the sheet with considerable interest.

His skills and abilities were average, or even below average.

The adventures he had completed consisted of: goblins, goblins, goblins, goblins, and more goblins.

I guess that explains why I've seen so few goblin-slaying quests left over recently.

"Keep piling up rocks and you get a mountain, huh?" she muttered to herself. She looked at Guild Girl with the sharp eyes of a cleric of the Supreme God. "You didn't forge any of this, did you?"

"As if I would do a thing like that!"

"Good, then." She nodded in acceptance.

Guild Girl, her chest puffed out proudly, could only smile ruefully.

Her colleague, finishing off the crust of her sandwich, winked at her.

"It's all good, anyway. Everyone meets one or two adventurers they'd like to encourage."

"Doesn't that contradict what you said earlier…?"

"Sometimes time and place dictate what you say."

"Whatever!"

Both of them started snickering.

Their break time would be over soon, and work would start again.

There were plenty of other adventurers up for promotion, too, meaning lots of paperwork to fill out.

"Since we're both here, how about we go out for a little drink tonight?"

"Sounds good. If I'm not too tired."

"All right, then. If you're not too tired." Guild Girl nodded with a smile and went back to her counter.

Her colleague disappeared for a moment but then poked her head back into Guild Girl's space.

"Hey, have people been calling that guy by some kind of nickname lately?"

"Yeah," Guild Girl said, looking as proud as if she were talking about her own achievements. "As a matter of fact, he…"

§

"Have you heard? There's this weird guy around these days."

"Oh, the one in that bizarre outfit?"

"The cheap-looking armor and helmet."

"The one who's always talking about goblins? I notice him every time he comes to the Guild."

"I mean, he's Porcelain, so what else is he gonna do?"

"Yeah, until he cuts his teeth…"

"Goblins are such a pain. If I never see another goblin, it'll be too soon."

"Come on, they can't be that bad. They're just goblins, right?"

"Anyway, what about him?"

"They say he's made Obsidian already."

"Wow, really? So was he part of that Rock Eater hunt?"

"No, I hear it's nothing but goblins for him."

"Do enough of them and I guess the experience adds up."

"Plus, he's solo."

"I heard one guy invited him on a different adventure, and he turned him down flat."

"He only ever hunts goblins, right?"

"Just goblins, goblins, goblins, goblins, huh?"

"So he's not a dragon slayer, he's…"

§

He didn't immediately realize the name referred to him.

He had finished making his report at the Guild and was just about to go outside.

The town bustled with activity, with eager voices. The rich summer sunlight shone all around.

He dismissed the way all these things flooded into his helmet and turned slowly around.

"Do you mean me?"

"Who else could I mean?"

The young warrior was standing there. The young man in the suit of armor had to think for a moment to recall who he was, but when he remembered, he nodded, the helmet moving quietly. "I see."

"Are your injuries better? I heard you got worked over by some goblins."

"Yes." He nodded again. "It's no problem."

It was all quite surprising: he had been completely exhausted, severely wounded, trudging through the rain before he finally collapsed.

He didn't know who had brought him to the temple, nor who had tended to his wounds. His injuries, however, healed miraculously well, his strength and stamina as good as they had ever been.

Normally, it would have taken many days to recover from something like that.

"Me too. We both need our health to make our living. I'm glad you're all right."

The young warrior gave him a pat on the shoulder. He thought for a moment, then the helmet tilted slowly.

"An adventure?"

"Yeah." The young man scratched the spot under his nose and laughed. "Slaying giant rats in the sewers."

"Is that so?"

"I don't have any party members anymore, but I figured I could solo for the time being."

There was still a hesitance about the young man, but the shrug he gave seemed natural enough.

He thought back to the image of the young warrior, his companions all gone, spending all his time in the tavern.

"...I see." He nodded, something the other man seemed to find somehow dazzling.

Then the young warrior gave the leather armor on his chest a friendly smack.

"If you're ever in trouble, call me."

"Um..."

"We registered on the same day. That's a bond."

He was silent for a moment, then said, "I understand." His voice was awkward and quiet as he added, "I'll do that."

"Sure thing," the young warrior said with a laugh, as though that answer pleased him somehow. "So what about you, then? More goblin slaying?"

"No." He shook his head slowly. "I was just going home."

He was just about to start walking again when he paused and said, "What was that you said to me? The first thing?"

"That?" the young warrior said, as if surprised he didn't already know. "It's a nickname."

"A nickname?"

"Sure." The young warrior grinned. "Your nickname.

"They call you Goblin Slayer."

§

"Er... Ergh..."

Cow Girl groaned, a bucket of water in front of her in her room.

Again and again, she put the scissors to her hair, which she could see reflected in the water.

But I d-don't have any idea how to cut my hair...

She had never given it much thought before, and now her lackadaisical approach had come back to haunt her. But it was too late now to wish that she had paid more attention to her bangs in the past.

She considered asking someone for help, but she was simply too embarrassed.

I mean... Come on...

It was all down to the reason she was cutting her hair.

That lady spell caster she had hired to be her bodyguard probably wouldn't have laughed at her to hear it, though.

I guess this isn't the sort of thing you ask an adventurer to help you with.

She had paid them to be her bodyguards; they weren't exactly her friends.

Cow Girl took a lock of her bangs between her fingers and brought the scissors to it, then pulled them back, agonizing over exactly what she should do.

"Oh, for..."

Bah! Just do it! Cow Girl screwed up her courage, then attacked her hair with the scissors.

Shink.

She heard the blades come together, and then a few strands of her bangs drifted down in front of her face.

She set the scissors aside and then tremblingly looked into the bucket. But...

"Hmm..."

For the life of her, she couldn't tell whether she had done a good job.

But I can't just leave it like this, that's for sure.

She had started this, and now she would have to finish it. With that thought filling her mind, she gave a little smirk.

He was the same way, she was sure.

"Okay!" Cow Girl said, smacking herself on the cheeks. Then she picked up the scissors again and began cutting boldly, slicing away swaths of her hair. As it fell, she felt like her head was getting lighter, her vision clearer.

Why did I leave it like that for so long?

It could almost have been funny to hear her wonder this; it had never bothered her before.

It was precisely realizing that fact that allowed her to become lighter like this. And that, she thought, was good.

"About like this, I guess...?"

She ran a hand through her hair, fiddled with her bangs, and then looked into the water again, muttering to herself.

It doesn't look...weird, does it?

She probably needed more practice. When her hair grew out again, she would take another stab at it.

With that thought, she cleaned up the bucket and scissors and swept up the hair with a broom.

A woman's hair was a precious thing; it could be sold for use in wigs or weaving or even to keep evil spirits away.

"A charm, huh?"

What if she were to give him something like that?

Nah... That'd be embarrassing.

Of course. And so, waving off her own idea, Cow Girl wrapped the collected hair carefully in oilpaper.

"Uh... Hmm..."

She couldn't quite bring herself to imagine handing it over to someone she didn't know, though. What was the best thing to do?

As she went back and forth—

"Yikes!"

—suddenly, she heard the sound of bold footsteps, a sound she had become accustomed to lately.

Cow Girl hurriedly tossed the hair onto a shelf, then ran a comb through the hair that was left on her head to straighten it before she went out to the front of the house.

What to say? Or rather, how to say it?

They had parted almost as if after a fight, and then she had gone and done this, and now...

She hardly knew what expression to make, let alone what words to use.

"Oh—"

But by the time all this had gone through her head, it was too late. There was a gentle clatter as the doorknob turned, and then the door opened with a soft creak.

The first thing she saw were his boots, which had gotten thoroughly covered in mud in the short time since he'd left.

The grimy leather armor, the cheap-looking steel helmet. The sword of a strange length at his hip, and the little round shield on his arm.

It was him.

He stopped there in the doorway and looked at her silently.

"Your hair…"

"Oh… Yeah."

Cow Girl found herself unable to avoid fidgeting as she stood there; her fingers tugged at the fringes of her hair.

"I cut it."

"Is that so?" He nodded once and was silent for a moment. Then he added, "I see."

It took him a while to come up with the response, but it was by no means as elaborate as Cow Girl was hoping. She expressed the dark feeling within herself by pursing her lips for a moment.

"Is that all?" she finally asked.

"Is what all?"

"Don't you have anything else to say? You know—*it looks good*, or, *that's so cute!*"

But, well…

Even if he had come up with those sentiments, she wouldn't have known how to react.

He didn't seem to know, either: after a while, the helmet shook slowly back and forth.

"I don't really know."

"I guess not," Cow Girl said, but then she smiled and added, "Can't be helped, can it?"

She twirled around and strolled toward the kitchen.

That was it—it couldn't be helped. It was just the way things were.

"It is not bad… At least, I think."

The voice was terribly soft and dispassionate, almost mechanical.

©Shingo Adachi

Cow Girl froze in her tracks.

She turned her head, with its newly shortened hair, and she let out a deep breath.

Then she turned her back on him again and said simply, "...Oh?"

"Yes."

That was all she needed. Those short, quiet words of his were all it took.

As she entered the kitchen, she spun around to face him.

"Hey," she said, putting both hands on the table and leaning forward. "Want me to make dinner for you?"

"......"

"It's stew. You'll eat it, right?"

Feelings are not as simple as words.

He didn't seem to know what to say.

The helmet remained silent, not offering even a ghost of a movement.

His expression was hidden behind his visor. Was he angry? Or not?

Cow Girl gulped—quietly, so he wouldn't notice.

Her hands grew tighter on the table.

A cow mooed outside.

She heard her uncle's voice far off, pursuing it.

Still, he hadn't answered her.

Still.

"...Yes."

"Great!"

Cow Girl clenched her fist in celebration the instant the helmet nodded in assent.

Then the tension drained out of her, her cheeks relaxing. Something that had been tight seemed to melt.

"Okay, I'll get started right away, then."

For the first time in a long time, she took up the apron that hung nearby. She hadn't done this since she was a child—at least five years ago.

She dimly remembered the recipes she'd learned. She wondered if she could still manage to make them. She should have practiced...

Well, never mind.

She would do it, starting now.

All of it. Everything. One thing at a time.

She had already cleaned. She would straighten up, do the laundry, and help out around the farm: all more and more things she'd do.

Even cooking—she would tackle it again and again. And he would eat what she made over and over.

"Oh, that's right."

She had forgotten something important.

She glanced at him from her spot in the kitchen. He had slumped awkwardly into a chair in the dining area.

She took a deep breath, holding it in that large chest of hers, and then said the words from which everything else would begin.

"Welcome home!"

Character Creation

Thus, the Adventurer Steps upon the Board

Clack, clack, roll, roll.

In the dimness of early twilight, the gods continue another day of playing eagerly at their dice.

The god called Abundance, his many tentacles squirming, is especially enjoying himself.

He's the one responsible for so greatly expanding the army of Chaos, creating unsolvable labyrinths and the like.

Yet somehow, the adventurers on the board, through tremendous effort, have managed to confront and overcome these things.

With great joy, Abundance rolls the dice, chuckling, "Heh-heh-heh! I'll get you back, I will!"

Some people say that gods are hardly gods who make sport of those living on this board.

But how do they expect to escape Fate and Chance?

Only the dice know all; thus, people are more than just playthings for those in the heavens.

The gods put genuine love into every throw of the dice.

Clack, clack, roll, roll.

Could those be Illusion and Truth rolling the dice over there?

It appears they're making new adventurers.

No maze, no matter how fabulous and terrifying, is more than an empty chamber without adventurers.

And of course, without powerful monsters to face, adventurers have no reason for being.

It looks like the result of all this die rolling is a warrior.

A human warrior, male. Vitality and skill points are decent; birth and life history typical.

He doesn't have all that much starting money. Nothing to complain about. Just average.

But he is who he is. And every adventurer is precious to the gods.

Illusion and Truth speak about what kinds of adventures this man will have once he's placed upon the board.

He'll start with goblin slaying, presumably. That's typical.

Some gods only let their adventurers muck out the sewers, claiming it's how adventuring really is. But that won't do.

Then they set about creating another new adventurer.

A lizardman priest, perhaps? A dwarf shaman might be fun as well.

And who could object to an elf archer? …Ah, good rolls. She turns out to be a high elf.

Clack, clack, roll, roll.

The gods are at their dice again today. What a wonderful time they're having.

These adventurers will go to dangerous places and fight hard to save the world.

At last, Truth, Illusion, and the other gods gather around Abundance.

You've got to win! Go—go, go, go! Rise, fight, kill! Gosh, you're awfully noisy.

Everyone cheers when their adventurer scores a critical hit, or cries out at the power of the dice.

Hence, none of the gods notice.

None of them notice what the warrior does.

No one in the whole world knows him yet.

Surely, the only ones who know about him are the dice Fate and Chance.

AFTERWORD

Hullo, Kumo Kagyu here!

How did you like *Goblin Slayer: Year One*?

It was the story of the first year Goblin Slayer slayed some goblins that had appeared.

I really put my heart and soul into this book, so I would be thrilled if you enjoyed it.

"Side Story"! When you say those words, it usually involves something like becoming a knight, but here we are.

I was actually really surprised when I was invited to do one.

I looked at my bookshelf, hoping for some inspiration, and saw a lot of *Year One* and *Returns* and *Gaslight*.

It's a bit too early for *Returns*, although I wouldn't mind doing a *Gaslight* story set in the nineteenth century.

But my dream was definitely *Year One*.

Every man wants to write a *Year One* story for the hero he created.

And so *Year One* it was. Hooray!

Goblin Slayer as we know him in the main series is already a seasoned adventurer. It was really fun writing the story of how he got his start as a level-one adventurer with no experience.

Plus, now that *Year One* is getting a manga adaptation, I can celebrate.

I guess it's really worth it, this struggle to live month to month.

Adachi-sensei, thank you so much for the illustrations. Cow Girl and Guild Girl look so innocent…!

Sakaeda-sensei, I'm so grateful for the manga version! Everyone is cute and sexy!

To my readers, thank you for all your support ever since my web novel days!

To all those who run the summary sites, thank you for always including my work.

To all my gaming friends, and all the other creative types in my life, thank you for the time you spend with me!

To all the editorial staff and everyone else involved with this book, thank you for all your help!

Novice adventurers always start out full of dreams. As they grow and mature, they want to do this and that, take down enemies and generally look cool, maybe get some treasure.

Each of them comes to adventuring with their own equipment, ideas, and philosophies.

That's very important and is something we should encourage and value.

Sometimes, the dice go against you and you die, but that's just the way it is.

If any of that came across in this book, even a little bit, then I've succeeded.

I hope I can communicate the same things in my next story.

I'll keep on putting everything I have into writing these books, so I hope you'll continue to read them.